THE
SECRET
WINNERS

THE
SECRET
WINNERS

by E. W. Hildick

Illustrated by
Gustave Nebel

© 1969 by E. W. Hildick. All rights reserved. No part of this book may be reproduced or utilized in any form or by any means, electronic or mechanical, including photocopying, recording, or by any other means, without permission in writing from the publisher.

Library of Congress Catalog Card Number:

Published simultaneously in Canada by Crown Publishing Company

CROWN PUBLISHERS, INC.   NEW YORK

Library of Congress Catalog Card Number: 74–113401

Published simultaneously in Canada by General Publishing Company Limited

To
Sophie Hardt

Also by E. W. Hildick

Manhattan Is Missing

Lemon Kelly

Jim Starling and the Colonel

Louie's Lot

Top Boy at Twisters Creek

Birdy Jones

Birdy and the Group

CONTENTS

CONTENTS

CHAPTER ONE

The Secret

"Ah, Tim, my boy—Tim, Tim, Timothy—come in, come in! How would you like to be having all the ice cream you could eat, eh? Every day when you get in all hot and ready for something cool, how would you like to dive into a bathtub full of ice cream and eat your way out, eh? . . . Come in, boy, come in—I've something to tell yez."

That was the way Tim O'Connell's uncle greeted him that afternoon. That was the way his Uncle James greeted him that hot afternoon when the sky hung heavy and yellow between the buildings.

At first Tim wondered if it was the heat. He knew that his uncle had lived in New York City most of his life—ever since he was a young man—and that the heat never seemed to bother him nowadays. But this was a specially hot and sticky day. And certainly Tim had never seen his uncle like this before: pacing up and down the room, the sweat trickling down all the long wrinkles in his thin, sad face, jabbering about ice cream, sounding much more Irish than he usually did, pacing there, pacing and jabbering away, still in his working clothes, still . . .

Still in his working *shoes*, for Pete's sake!

Tim stared at the man's feet. As he bent to unfasten his own shoes, he stared at his uncle's feet as they paced up and down and he decided that he must have guessed right first time. The heat really had gotten to his uncle. Must have. Maybe he'd been working on an outside job, repair-

ing some electrical fault out under the full weight of the
heat. Maybe his boss had kept him going just that little
bit too fast out there, and he'd cracked. Why else should
he be home at this time, before five o'clock? And why else
should he be wearing his outdoor shoes in the apartment?

"Your shoes, Uncle James—aren't you gonna take
them off?"

"Shoes? Shoes?" The man stopped in his tracks and
stared at Tim. "Shoes? Sure I'll buy you some shoes. Any
kind you like. The best there is. Brown ones, black ones,
black and yaller ones like the kind I always wanted when
I was your age. Moccasins, if you like. Genuine Indian
moccasins. Or them things that curl up in front, like in
Turkey. Just you name 'em, my boy, and I'll have a
messenger bring 'em around—a pair for each day of the
week and two for Sundays. . . . Only stop fooling
around and come on in. I've news for yez."

Then Tim *knew* his uncle must have gone crazy. The
man didn't even know what he was doing. He didn't even
realize he was still wearing his shoes! In there! In the
apartment! With Aunt Bridget due back any time now
from the last of her day's cleaning sessions. . . .

He slipped off his own shoes and put them in the
special rack by the door. Then he padded across to the
corner by the window, where the tiny electric fan was
turning slowly, battling every inch of the way.

Uncle James nodded.

"That's it, my boy. Get where it's cooler, ready to
receive the news I have to tell you. I know how you feel
about the heat. It took me twenty years after we got over
from Belfast to get accustomed to it, and you've been here
only a year now . . ."

"Two, Uncle—two. I'm twelve, remember. I came on
my tenth birthday. Two years and three weeks."

"As long as that, is it? Sure, of course! The way time
flies . . ."

Tim began to feel better. This sounded more like the usual Uncle James: sad, sighing—but sane. He'd even stopped pacing about and was sitting in the flower-patterned armchair.

"The sheet, Uncle," Tim gently reminded him.

"Eh?"

"The sheet. For the chair."

He waved toward the clothes closet where Aunt Bridget kept the old sheet she made them drape over the flower-patterned chair whenever they sat in it—even in their best clothes.

Uncle James gave a twitch. Then a snort. Then a great crack of a laugh.

"The divil take the sheet, my boy!" he cried, leaping up and starting to pace again. "And the chair with it! We'll buy her a new one every day. We'll buy her chair covers by the gross, the best there is, silk ones, covers of the finest linen old Belfast ever turned out, and she can use 'em like paper towels. She can throw 'em away like paper towels."

Tim didn't bother to point out that Aunt Bridget didn't care much for paper towels. He didn't bother to remind his uncle that when she did use paper towels she rarely threw them away first go, but put them carefully in a special box for use as window cloths. For his uncle was jabbering away again, faster than before, flinging his arms about as he paced and—horror of horrors—doing a little dance every few steps! In his work shoes! Scuffing the thin but carefully placed and spotlessly clean rug here, scratching the polished varnish on the wooden floor there . . .

"Please, Uncle, *please* sit down! You'll only get hotter than ever."

"Hotter? Heat? What's that matter *now*, my boy? I was just beginning to tell you, before you sidetracked me with all that baloney about sitting on sheets—we can afford air-conditioning in every corner of the apartment now. Every room. Air-conditioning such as you never dreamed of. Instead of fixing air-conditioners, I'll be using 'em. Think of that! With beautiful perfumes running through at the same time as the cool air: violets, new-mown hay, marshmallow smells, strawberry, peanut brittle—any smell you fancy, no need to stick to flowers. And music also—fiddle music, guitars, drums, trumpets, just as the mood takes you, dial the one you want. Me, I'd be dialing a nice little jig right now, with a whiff of mountain pines, at a setting of about seventy-one degrees, which I find very comfortable when dancing. . . ."

"But Aunt Bridget—"

"In winter of course it will be different. Then we'll have warm air blowing through, with roast-chestnut smells and the smell of fine cigars—"

"Aunt Bridget'll be back any minute and—"

"And the music for winter, well, we'll still have jigs and reels, but carols also. You know, something seasonal, and—and . . ." Slowly the man's words began to tail off. Slowly the light left his eyes. Slowly he sank back into the armchair. Slowly he slumped, head in hands. "Ah!" he sighed. "To be sure. . . . There's your Aunt Bridget. . . . I keep forgetting. . . ." He looked up. "Tim," he said, "we got to think of something. We got to think of a way of breaking it to her. You'll help me in this now, won't you?"

"Break *what* to her, Uncle? What are you talking about?"

"The news."

"*What* news?"

"The secret."

"*What* secret?"

"Our secret, my boy."

Uncle James nodded slowly. Then he shook his head and slapped his leg.

"Blow me down!" he cried. "I'd clean forgot I hadn't told you already!" He got up and went to the door. He even remembered to heel off his shoes this time and place them in the rack. Then, after peering into the corridor, he carefully closed the door. "Never mind about a through draft for a minute," he whispered, going over to the closet and taking out the dust sheet for the chair. "This is dynamite. I don't want one breath of this secret to reach your Aunt Bridget's ears till we've figured out what to do."

He carefully placed the sheet over the chair, as if the very flowers in the pattern had ears to hear with, and tongues to pass on to their mistress whatever they heard.

"The fact is, my boy," said Uncle James, dropping his voice so low that Tim had to stretch forward, away from the hum of the fan and the rumble of street noises, "the plain fact is that we're rich, you and me. We just won half a million dollars. . . ."

CHAPTER TWO

The Problem

"A—HALF a *million?*"

Uncle James nodded. He winced as he nodded.

"Keep it down, boy! The voice! Please!"

"Half a million *dollars?*" whispered Tim.

"Genuine American dollars, yes."

"You mean—?"

"I mean the lottery ticket we bought, last May. The one I let you buy into for a nickel. The ticket that cost a dollar—ninety-five cents me, five cents you. Yes."

"Which? Which one? Which ticket was it, Uncle?"

Uncle James winced again.

"Please! Whatever happens, never let your aunt know I'm in the *habit* of buying lottery tickets. And above all—now listen to me, my boy—above *all*, never let her know that I let you in on buying a ticket from time to time."

Uncle James was entirely his usual self again, talking out of the side of his mouth, looking hunted, worried, but with an occasional quick smile for Tim. One flitted across his face now.

"You sure brought us luck with that nickel!"

Now it was Tim's turn to jump up.

"But this is *great* news, Uncle!"

"The *voice!*" groaned Uncle James.

"But it *is!*" whispered Tim, still jumping. "We can buy all sorts of things. We can move apartments. We can have a car. Aunt Bridget won't have to go out working anymore! *You* won't. . . ."

"I know, I know. . . . But—"

"But what, Uncle?"

"But how do we *explain* it, boy? How do we break it to your aunt. *You* know what she's like. You know what she thinks of such things. You know how I daren't even smoke in the house, or drink a can of beer. Or tell tales, even— even that she doesn't like me doing. Simple little old fairy tales she says is nothing better than a pack of lies. . . . As for *gambling* . . ."

Uncle James groaned and hung his head again.

Tim sat down and hung his. He was beginning to see.

"You know what she'd do?" said Uncle James. "She'd make us give it all back. That's what she'd do."

"But half a million dollars!"

"Makes no difference. Least, the difference would be this: She'd be all the more set against it. The bigger the prize, the bigger the sin."

"But what if they say they won't take the money back? That it's none of their business anymore?"

For a second Uncle James looked up hopefully. Then he slumped again.

"No difference. She'd only make us turn it all over to charity."

"We could give *some* of it to charity, I suppose. We'd be doing that anyway, wouldn't we?"

"Sure! Sure! But your aunt would insist on the *lot* going to charity. If you 'n' me took so much as a bag of popcorn for ourselves we'd never hear the end of it. . . ." The man sighed heavily again. " 'Course, some guys would just tell her to go jump in a lake. Some guys if they won all that would say she'd better get used to the idea or go and be miserable all on her own."

"Oh, but Aunt Bridget, she—"

"I know, my boy, I know. She preaches at us, she bullies us, she acts like we was a pair of bums or hippies or something. She won't let us wear shoes in the apartment or sit comfortable on a chair, and she's a heller when it comes to making rules. *I've* had this thirty years. I ought to know. . . . But you're right, my boy. She's good enough at heart. She can be real sweet at heart—like—like milk in some tough old coconut."

"And she does worry about us."

"And nothing's too much trouble when we're sick. Yeah. I know, I know. . . ."

"And she works very hard."

"And she loves you like you was her own son."

"So we can't just leave her, can we, Uncle?"

"Who said anything about *leaving* her? I just said *some* guys would. Most guys . . . no. But at the same time we can't go telling her how we came by the money."

Tim frowned.

"Won't she find out anyhow? Won't it be in the papers? On television?"

Uncle James drew a deep breath.

"It will *not!* Remember I filled out that No Publicity bit on the ticket stub? Asking to remain what-d'ye-call-it, if the Good Lord should see fit to bless us with the winning number . . ."

"Anonymous."

"Eh?" Uncle James jumped up, startled.

"Anonymous," said Tim. "That's the word for when you don't want folks to know your name."

"Oh!" grunted his uncle, sitting down again. "I thought you said your aunt was coming or something. . . . Anyhow, the thing is this: We got to figure out a way of making it look as if we came by the money some way she doesn't object to. Right? . . . Right. Well, you be thinking, my boy, because I've always said you got a good head on them shoulders. . . . Meantime, I have a call to make. I want to fix it so the check's paid into a bank someplace well out of this neighborhood, some-where over on Fifth Avenue, where there'll be nobody to

see us when we draw out a hatful of dollars from time to
time. Nobody who knows us, that is. Because whatever
we do—"

Uncle James put on his battered old hat with the wilting wide brim.

"—whatever we do, we mustn't let the news get back
to your aunt before we're ready for her."

He slipped his shoes on at the door.

"And remember: *You* keep quiet about it, Tim. Don't
breathe a word of it to a single living soul, man or beast.
Okay?"

"Okay," said Tim.

With a little scuffle of the feet, betraying that his
spirits were rising again at the thought of all that money
—problem or no problem—Uncle James went out, whis-
tling softly to himself.

It was the tune of "Bryan O'Lynn"—one of the many
songs that Aunt Bridget strongly objected to, and, as Tim
listened to it fading, he remembered just why she dis-
approved of it. The word *breeches*. It contained the line,
"Bryan O'Lynn had no breeches to wear." Tim could
almost hear her voice now, saying, "That's enough of *that*
disgusting language, James O'Connell!" It made him
realize all the more how important it was to keep the
news of their big win from a woman as straitlaced as that.

He slipped on his shoes and went out into the street
himself, suddenly scared that she might walk in while the
news was still hot inside him, blazing there, a five-hun-
dred-thousand-dollar furnace, with the light of it shining
out from behind his eyes.

CHAPTER THREE

The Temptation

OUT IN THE STREET it didn't seem to Tim as hot and heavy as it had half an hour ago. The hazy yellow sky still hung between the buildings; the old yellow dog on the stoop by the door still found it hard to lift a leg to scratch his fleas; and people were still moving slowly, carefully, as if on the lookout for any sudden breeze that might spring up, anxious for a breath of it before it wafted away again.

But to Tim it was different now. Maybe it was because of the secret burning inside him—that half-a-million-dollar furnace there—making anything that came from outside seem cool by comparison. Right now his feet would have felt like skipping even if he'd been wearing moon-walker's boots.

For, once outside the apartment, he forgot all about the problem of breaking the news to Aunt Bridget. Away from the shoe rack by the door, the polish, the smell of strong soap, the dust sheets, and all the other reminders of her presence, he could think only of those dollars and everything they were able to buy.

So he saw the old yellow dog and thought about the beautiful Saint Bernard he and Uncle James could get now if they wanted. The beautiful Saint Bernard they used to talk about (when Aunt Bridget wasn't listening) ever since they'd watched a mountaineering movie on television. The beautiful Saint Bernard with a little barrel hanging from its collar. ("Filled with Irish whiskey, my boy, not your ould French brandy. Irish whiskey, which can revive men from the dead—and we'll tell your aunt it's only a drop of root beer, and train him to growl whenever she puts out a hand to check on the fact.")

So—aglow with the burning dollars—Tim saw the parked Cadillac of the superintendent at the apartment building opposite. It was ten years old, with a buckled fender and a rear door so battered it wouldn't ever open again, yet it was the envy of the neighborhood, Tim and his uncle included. Well, now it looked like what it was. It looked like nothing more than a heap of junk with a *fairly* good engine, as Tim thought of the big gleaming brand-new silvery Rolls Royce they could buy that very afternoon, if they cared to.

So—seeing Terry Noone and some of the other kids hanging around a fire hydrant, trying to get it to gush with the aid of an old wrench—Tim thought of the swimming pool he and his uncle could now afford, and the house and the gardens to go with it.

"Hey, Tim! C'm on over and gimme a hand with this, will ya?"

Tim hardly heard the cry, as he wandered on, down the street. All he did was wave and murmur something about an Olympic diving board, as he went on thinking about those dollars and the things he could buy. Mountains of pure ice cream rose up at the sight of a wrapper in the gutter. The boom of a jet reminded him of the trips he would now be able to take: to Ireland, to Italy, to Africa, to Australia, to India. And one thing led to another. The ice-cream mountains reminded him of his favorite peanut brittle, which he need never go short of again; and the trips by jet reminded him of the shorter but equally marvelous trips they could now take by car to places like Playland and Bear Mountain and the J. F. Kennedy Airport itself.

"Hey! You gone deaf or somethin'?"

Tim stopped and turned to see Terry Noone scowling at him from across the street, looking ready to throw the wrench at him. Tim smiled. He liked Terry. Terry never smiled at anyone—not at any of the other kids, anyway— and somehow that made you want to *try* getting him to smile. Any other afternoon, Tim would have gone across and wrestled with that hydrant along with the others, hoping to produce the gush of water that might—just might—bring a grin to that thin, fierce, freckled face. But today he forced himself to move on. He knew that if he went across there he might not be able to keep the secret, that the news of those dollars might gush out long before the old hydrant coughed up its water.

So he went on his way.

But now a new thing was happening. Now that he'd *thought* of unleashing the secret, he found himself wanting to—aching to. He couldn't stop thinking of it—bursting to get out like the water in the hydrant—and it was making him ache. He found himself lingering in front of people—grown-ups as well as kids, people he knew well and others he knew only a little. In front of old Larry, the car jockey, sitting on his chair outside the parking garage, he lingered, and if Larry hadn't been fast asleep, if he'd opened just one eye and said, as he usually did, "Hello, Irish, what's new today?" the secret would have been out.

Tim realized this, and it gave him a little shock. He tried hard to think of nothing but his Uncle James's anxious face as the man uttered the warning: "Don't breathe a word of it to a single living soul, man or beast!"

And this gave him an idea.

Uncle James was always saying things like that, exaggerating like that. For instance, the bit about "man or beast." All right, the "man" part figured. People could talk. Tell *them* your secret and there was always the risk they'd pass it on. But "beast"? What harm was there in

telling an animal, for Pete's sake? At least it might do
something to relieve the pressure, and *they'd* never be
able to pass on the details, that was for sure.

Tim looked around, and the first animal he saw was a
cat—a thin black cat prowling around the side of some
empty garbage cans.

"Hey, puss, listen, puss!" he hissed, crouching beside
it, his head near the cat's. "I've got some marvelous news."

The cat was an old neighborhood cat. It had had lots
of experience with the neighborhood kids. It arched its
back and spat at him, then went off growling, ears flat, to
glare at him from under a parked car.

The next cat he tried was more docile. It was a
younger, fatter cat, striped gray and black, and it came to
his call with its tail up, ready to talk. It even rolled on its
back with joy at his good news, which he whispered as he
scratched it down its front. But somehow this didn't give
him the relief that he wanted. The secret still pressed and
pushed inside him as he went on his way, and he decided
that this was because cats were such quiet secret creatures themselves. They probably knew your secrets just
looking at you, just picking up your thoughts on those
whiskers of theirs, like radio antennae. There wasn't much
fun in actually telling *them*. . . .

So then he switched to dogs and at first this was
better. The little black-and-white terrier tethered to a post
outside the supermarket yapped with joy and wagged its
tail at the news Tim whispered in its ear. Mrs. Gruber's
basset hound listened intently and grunted some good
advice or other. And even the old yellow dog back at the
building stopped its attempts to scratch, opened both eyes
and gave a little whimper of pleasure.

Then dogs too began to seem unsatisfactory. Barks,
grunts, whimpers—these were better than nothing, sure,
and they showed the animal understood that something

good was being talked about. But it wasn't like having a real voice say in real English:

"Gee! That's terrific news, Tim! What ya gonna buy first with it?"

Now by this time Tim was ready to go back into the building. And everything might have been all right if he'd done just that: if he'd patted the old dog's head, stepped over it and gone indoors. But the thought of a human voice reminded him of one "beast" that possessed one—Mrs. Hennessy's talking bird, the parrot that on fine days was hung in its cage from her window, just around the block.

"Hey! Bird! I got a secret!" Tim was whispering, two minutes later.

It wasn't a very soft whisper, since the bottom of the cage was still a good three feet above his head even when he stood, straddle-legged, on the sloping wall of the stoop at the side. But luckily there was no one else sitting there or playing there just at the moment.

"Bird! D'you hear me? I got a secret."

The parrot fluttered its wings a little and bent its head. It seemed to be saying, "Yeah! I hear ya. And I'm a good judge of secrets, feller, so this had better be good!"

Tim carried on as if these had been the parrot's exact spoken words.

"Well, listen. I bet you never heard one like this before. My uncle and—"

"Boy! You teaching that bird to swear? I'm sick to death of the way you kids got nothin' better to do 'n teach an innocent creature foul words, and if you don't clear off . . ."

As he ran away along the street, Tim didn't know whether to be mad at the interruption or glad that the woman had stopped him in time before she could hear what he was really saying. All he did know was that the secret was pressing stronger than ever, was pressing to

bursting point, and that if he didn't get back home quick he'd be shouting it out to every passerby: man, woman, child, dog, cat, bird, insect. . . .

Then: "Hi, Tim! You wanner come to the supermarket with me?"

It was Terry Noone. He was alone now. It seemed as if he'd given up trying to get the hydrant to work, or had been chased away, or had been called in by his mother to run this errand. Anyway, Terry was looking friendlier than he'd looked for days, Tim noticed. The other boy was almost *smiling* even, and all at once Tim knew that *this* was the one he must tell his news to.

"No. I better be going in now, Terry. But listen—," he added hurriedly, seeing a jeer begin to spread itself across the other's face "—listen, Terry, I got a wonderful secret. Promise you won't—"

Terry was already nodding impatiently. "Okay! Okay! Let's hear it. Cut out the crossing-the-heart bit and let's hear it. I won't tell."

"Well . . . my uncle and me, we bought this ticket. It cost a dollar and I chipped in with a nickel. . . ."

Nodding, grunting, sniffing, scratching, Terry Noone listened. At first he seemed only mildly interested. Then his eyes grew wider and wider. For once it seemed as if he were going to grin with delight, actually smile at another kid, at *him*, Tim O'Connell. For once it seemed that Terry Noone was going to admit that something great could happen to some other kid.

"So? . . . So? . . . So? . . . C'm on? How much you win then? Twenty bucks? Maybe fifty, eh? Not a *hunret?*"

Slowly Tim shook his head and smiled. The surging secret inside him was now all ready to spill out in all its splendor: a Niagara Falls of a secret.

"Twenty? Fifty? A hundred? Are you kidding, man? Me and my uncle, we won half a million. Dollars."

For a second, Terry Noone looked stunned. It looked as if he really had been standing under Niagara Falls the time it was turned off, and they'd switched the water on again without letting him know. He looked stunned. He looked as if all the breath had been knocked out of him.

Then his face broke open in what looked for a moment like a grin, but soon turned out to be a jeer.

"You nuts or somethin'?" he cried, at the top of his voice. "You expect me to believe *that?* . . . Hey! Charlie! Sharon! Burt! C'm over here an' listen to this," he continued, for the whole block to hear. "Tim O'Connell's tryna tell me him and his uncle won half a million bucks!"

CHAPTER FOUR

The Betrayal

EVEN BEFORE he'd got back into the apartment, Tim realized what he had done. Even as he was shrugging his shoulders and turning his back on the jeering Terry, he knew he had betrayed the secret. It was true that Terry and the other kids had refused to believe him, but that made no difference. He had done exactly what Uncle James had asked him not to do.

By the time Tim got in, his uncle was already back. He was pacing up and down in front of the window in his stockinged feet. He had forgotten to take his hat off, Tim noticed, but his shoes he had remembered. He was obviously still just as excited about the win, and just as worried about Aunt Bridget.

"Ah, it's you, my boy, it's you!" he cried, spinning around and then sitting down in the flowered chair with the sort of thump that would have rated a half-hour lecture from his wife, had she seen him. "Your aunt's late today. Maybe it's as well. We've got to keep calm, keep cool. We've got to behave like everything's normal until we can figure a way out of this."

Tim drew a deep breath. His face was scarlet—he could feel it on his cheeks. But at least Uncle James hadn't heard Terry Noone's cry come curling over the rooftops and down through the open window. Tim uncrossed his fingers and for once felt grateful that the window didn't face the street.

"Did—did you make your call, Uncle? Is it okay about the bank?"

"Eh? . . . Oh, sure, sure! *That* was no problem. We now have a checking account at the New Era Benefit Bank on Fifth Avenue. With a lawyer feller to advise on handling the dough and any tax problems and suchlike." Uncle James shot up from the chair and began pacing again. "But we still haven't thought of a way of getting the stuff out and spending it freely. And there ain't a lawyer born to advise us on *that,* far as I can see."

He clutched at his head, probably meaning to claw through his thin strands of hair the way he often did when he was upset. Finding his hat in the way, he snatched it off and hurled it to the floor—still pacing—and he kicked it under the sofa out of the way when he got up to it.

"Great glorious heavens above!" he cried, coming to a halt at the wall and staring up at the old brown photograph of Aunt Bridget's grandmother—the only picture she'd allow in the house, on account of their being such "dust traps," as she called them. "Great good glorious heavens above!" cried Uncle James, as if his wife's ancestor were his only contact with that region. "Here we are—rich! rich! rich!—and we have to go skulking about like a pair of crooks, pretending we ain't got nothing but what we earn working!"

Then he turned again, and it was as if the grim-faced old lady with the high collar up there had uttered a sharp practical reminder.

"Now you sure you can keep it a secret, boy?" he said.

Tim swallowed. He looked down from his uncle's anxious peering eyes to the pair of big toes poking out through the man's socks.

"I—er—sure—I—".

And he was just picking up a little speed, having told himself that it wasn't *exactly* lying to say he could keep it a secret, *from now on,* when the door handle was rattled briskly and in stepped Aunt Bridget.

In many ways it was just like her usual homecoming. First came the brisk rattle. Then came the dumping of her big old shabby black pocketbook and a sack of groceries on the chair at the side of the door. It was a chair reserved especially for such packages and it always reminded Tim of the bench in the customs hall, when he'd first entered the country—giving him a very uneasy feeling whenever the packages were something *he* was bringing in.

Then, with a long sad sigh, came the easing off of Aunt Bridget's shoes and their placing in the rack. After that, it was the glances—the fusillade of sharp glances she would flash around the room like sniper's bullets. Some might be aimed at other people's feet, to check on why certain shoes weren't already on the rack. Some were always aimed at the table and the floor around the table, for any traces of cookies or other foodstuff that might have been consumed, against all rules, before the proper time. The glance at the television set was another routine shot: to see from the position of the antennae ears (which had always to be kept neatly buttoned down when the set was not in use) whether Tim or her husband had dared to dally with "that devil's machine" before the six o'clock news program.

And it wasn't just glances, either. There were the sniffs, too, coming between the glances, as she sought for traces of illicit tobacco or bubble gum or even coffee— none of which she would allow into the apartment.

But then would usually come the best part. If everything was as it should be she would smile—and it was a lovely smile to see. Her long, bony, tired, suspicious face would suddenly relax, her eyes would widen so that you could see what a beautiful violet blue they really were,

and her still-white, still-strong teeth (brushed three times
a day, ten minutes a time) would shine out. It was like the
sun coming out over the sea, Tim always thought. It was
like the sun coming out over the sea after a storm cloud
has passed, sparkling on the white-capped waves that had
looked so grim and threatening a moment ago.

Tonight, however, there was no such smile. And it
wasn't as if she'd caught sight of Uncle James's hat, kicked
so recklessly and untidily under the sofa.

No.

It was Tim she was looking at.

"Now then," she said, in a voice that made his toes
wriggle in their socks, "what's all this about winning a
lottery prize?"

From over by the window there came a faint moan
and a twanging crash as Uncle James slumped straight
down into the flowered chair—and on any other occasion
it would have earned him a *three*-hour lecture and a week
in the doghouse. This time it didn't cause so much as a
flicker in the narrow angry gaze that was trained on Tim.

"Well?"

Tim closed his eyes. He couldn't take it any longer.
Much as he dreaded his aunt's wrath, he was dreading
even more the look that he knew would be there in the
eyes of the man on the chair behind him. If—at that
moment—the old lady on the wall had come to life,
reached out and yanked him by the hair up into her grim
brown heaven, he would have been grateful.

But the tug came from bonier, stronger fingers.

"Look at me, Timothy! I asked you a question. I said
what's all this I been hearing—about you winning a prize
with a lottery ticket?"

"A lu-lu-lottery ticket?" came the weak gasp from the
flowered chair.

"I'll thank you to hold your tongue for once, James
O'Connell. I'll be talking to you in a minute. I suspect this

soft-brained rubbishy mish-mash started with *you.* . . .
But first—" she gave Tim's hair another tug "—I want to
hear what you've been telling that young Terry Watsis-
name over the street."

"Terry Noone?"

"The name doesn't matter. The story does. I happened
to hear him blethering it all over the supermarket just ten
minutes ago. What is it all about?"

"I—well—I—well, I told him we'd bought this lottery
ticket—"

"*We?*"

"Let me explain, my dear—"

"You keep out of this, Mr. O'Connell, if you please!"

At that, Uncle James's groan rose into a bleat before
he fell silent. When his wife addressed him as "Mr.
O'Connell" it meant he was in the worst possible trouble.

"Go on."

"Well—I—I told him me and my uncle, my uncle and
me, and *I*, we bought this ticket and we won this prize.
This—this half a million dollars," Tim added, hopeful that
the size of the win might after all give her different,
happier ideas about gambling. "Five hundred thousand."

"American dollars, Bridie, my dear," breathed Uncle
James, obviously hoping for the same break.

This time Aunt Bridget ignored him completely. Still
gazing at Tim, she nodded her head.

"Yes!" she said. "That was exactly as I heard it. And a
fine story it was to have blethered all around your neighborhood store, about your own nephew who is like your
own son, and about your own husband who puts such
ideas into the boy. A *fine* story, a very fine story indeed!
. . . Well now, you just listen to me, the both of yez. I
want to hear no more of such drivel—either from your-
selves direct or through the mouth of some other person.
Do you understand? Because it's dreams and fairy tales
like that as'll get you nowhere, boy, understand?—no-

where—where your Uncle James is after all these years of
dreams and fairy tales. It's only *work* that'll get you
somewheres—hard work, real work, steady work—and
going to bed early and getting up early, and living clean,
and looking after your health. *That's* what'll get you
somewheres, if the Good Lord gives his approval. Understand?"

Tim nodded, trying not to show how relieved he was
that she too hadn't believed his story. And:

"Your aunt's right, my boy," came Uncle James's murmur, with something in his tone that showed he was
feeling pretty much the same. "She—"

"As for you, Mr. O'Connell—as for you, Mr. James
Oscar Errol O'Connell—I consider you to be more to
blame than the boy himself—not that *he's* not old enough
to be knowing better. I think it's a crying disgrace that as
soon as my back's turned you start in stuffing his head
with ideas that'll come to a boy soon enough in this Sinful
City without any help from you. . . ."

So she went on. And on. And on.

And so they listened in silence, for once secretly glad
to let her go on, readier to listen to a fifty-thousand-word
sermon—even a five-hundred-thousand-word sermon—
than be forced to answer any more awkward questions.

CHAPTER FIVE

The Plan

It was on the very next day that Uncle James had the first of his "foolproof ideas."

He had set off for work at the usual time, about fifteen minutes before Aunt Bridget was due to leave for the first of her cleaning sessions. But he had not left the apartment without pressing into Tim's hand a tightly screwed ball of paper bearing the message:

BE ON HAND, MY BOY, AT 9:15 A.M.,
WHEN I'LL BE BACK. DESTROY THIS
OR ALL IS LOST.

So Tim, after flushing the message down the toilet and seeing his aunt leave for work, had waited impatiently in the apartment. He was glad that at least it was the long summer vacation, when he could give his whole mind to the problem, yet he was doubtful whether Uncle James would have managed to come up with a solution so early.

However, his uncle certainly looked much happier than he had the previous day, when, dead on the stroke of 9:15, he arrived back.

"My boy," he said, without bothering to take off either hat or shoes, "get your sneakers on—we're in business."

"You mean—?"

"I mean your old uncle spent a sleepless night last night but not for nothing. The O'Connells ride again, my boy. I've had me a foolproof idea, the solution to all our problems in this world and the next. And by the way, I've just called the boss and quit my job."

"You've quit your job?"

"Sure, sure! And why not, when I'm worth the best part of five hundred thousand dollars. It would take me nearly a hundred years to earn all that—not counting taxes—so why should I go on slaving away? That, at least, the prize has earned me. . . . But listen, boy, that's not the point. The point is that I've had me a foolproof idea for bringing home *some* of the money, just for starters."

Tim had slipped on his sneakers. There was something about the tone of his uncle's voice, and the flush on his cheeks, and the sparkle in his eyes, and the set of his shoulders, and the turn of his wrists, that convinced the boy he really had a good idea.

"And what it is, is this," continued Uncle James, actually putting a foot on the unsheeted flower chair and leaning forward and resting his elbow on his knee. "I want you to go out and find me an old receptacle."

"A—?"

"A box or something. Something to put something in when you want to stash something away. A box, boy—or listen, a sock. That's it. An old sock. A box'll do but a sock would be ideal, because that's what folks generally do put their dough in when they're stashing it away."

"But what dough, Uncle?"

"The dough we're gonna *find,* my boy. Me and you. Right this very day."

"You mean some of the money we've won?"

"You're bright, my boy. Really bright. Just like your poor father, God rest his soul. Yes."

Tim grinned.

"I *see,* now. . . . We're gonna pretend we've found it—"

"Some of it. Not all. Just some of it. For starters. A thousand, I thought. That would be nice to be going on with, would it not?"

Tim was nodding. But he was frowning now, also.

"Yes, but Aunt Bridget—she'll only make us turn it over to the police."

Uncle James laughed. He took off his hat and swatted at a fly on his knee.

"*Sure* she will! But listen. . . . *We* know nobody's really lost it, don't we? And when nobody claims it, well, whoever finds it can have it back. That's the law."

Tim was still frowning.

"But don't you have to wait for months before they hand it over?"

"Months? I thought it was weeks. But anyway, what does it matter? In the end we get it back and your aunt's got nothing to complain about, and we get to spend it freely. . . . As I was saying, it's a start, my boy. And it's foolproof."

"Yes," said Tim, cheering up. "And even if we do have to wait a few months, we should get it in time for Christmas. Why, we could buy Aunt Bridget a pearl necklace out of it."

"I was thinking a pair of good stout shoes might be more welcome in that quarter. And a winter coat—a real good one. But as you say, we should be able to reclaim it in time for Christmas. *If* we get started right away. . . ."

Tim could take a hint, and, while Uncle James went over to Fifth Avenue to draw the money from the bank, he went on a tour of the neighborhood garbage cans.

It took him nearly an hour before he found what he was looking for. In that time he came across boxes of all sizes: wooden ones, plastic ones, cardboard ones, and two metal ones, both with broken lids but otherwise serviceable. He also found several kinds of sacks, ranging from paper to jute, some of them impossibly greasy or torn but one or two that would have been just right. Even so, Uncle James had obviously set his heart on a sock, and so—in Tim's reckoning—a sock it had to be.

Now on any ordinary day, had he just been passing by

the garbage cans, he'd probably have spotted any number
of discarded socks and stockings. He told himself this,
more than once, as he searched away in the steadily
growing heat of the morning sun. "Nylons, knee socks, red
socks, green socks—any other day I'd be seeing nothing
but lousy socks spilling over the edges. But today—no!"

In fact, he was beginning to wonder whether to settle
for an old shoe of some sort—for, to give it its due, it was
an excellent day for shoes—when he spotted it.

He could hardly believe his eyes.

There, full in a shaft of morning sunlight, lying at the
side of a can, simply begging to be seen and claimed, and
only two blocks away from the apartment, was a sock that
seemed to have been specially made to take a thousand
dollars in bills: a real true, right royal money-stasher of a
sock.

Basically it was purple—the color of kings and luxury
living. And it had a pattern of yellow stripes, the color of
pure gold, in a crisscross arrangement that reminded Tim
of a picture of the bars in front of the Caliph's treasure
house in an Arabian Nights storybook.

On somebody's foot it might have looked a little too
loud, which was probably the reason for its being thrown
away (for it certainly had no holes in it, and only two
small patches of darning, in a bright green wool that
made it look louder still); yet as a—what was Uncle
James's word?—as a *receptacle,* a receptacle for a thousand dollars, it was perfect.

Feeling almost as guilty as if the sock itself had been
worth that much money, Tim looked around carefully,
snatched it up, gave it a flick against the side of the can to
get rid of some of the dust that was sticking to it, and
stuffed it under his shirt. . . .

That evening, they told Aunt Bridget about it. Not
everything about it, of course—but everything about it

that they wanted her to know.

"It was just lying around with the rest of the litter."

"The boy was attracted by its colors, he tells me."

"All purply, with gold crisscrosses."

"He has an eye for colors and patterns, like his poor dear mother—"

"Be quiet, James, and let him tell it himself."

"And—and I picked it up—"

"You should *never* pick up things like that."

"Yes, I know, Aunt. But this—well—"

"It was different, Bridget. This was something else again."

"Will you be *quiet*, James! . . . Go on, Timothy."

"And—well—I found it was full of this money."

(At this point, Tim crossed his fingers and hoped his aunt wouldn't question him more closely and find out that the money came later—after he'd taken the sock in triumph to his uncle.)

"Yes, yes, go on. What did you do *then?*"

"I took it to the police station, ma'am."

As he said this, Tim looked her straight in the eye, actually feeling proud of himself. For that was exactly what he *had* done—after Uncle James had carefully stowed away inside it the bundles of twenty-dollar bills, pushing the first ones down to the very toe space.

Aunt Bridget gave one of her glorious sunny smiles. This was the third time around for her—and each time she heard the story her smile grew wider.

"I'm very glad to hear it, Timothy," she said. "That's exactly what you should have done."

"I didn't even stop to count it," said Tim, feeling as pleased and proud as if it had all happened as she imagined it, and hoping for another smile.

Instead, his aunt's face clouded for a moment.

"But I hope you made them count it at the station house?" she said, for she was no fool, and liked things done as legally as possible.

"Oh, sure!" said Uncle James. "Of course he did, my dear. The boy's not an O'Connell for nothing. . . . There was one thousand, Tim, wasn't there?"

"Exactly," said Tim. "Exactly a thousand."

"Well," said Aunt Bridget, "let's hope the poor soul it belongs to finds out and claims it for his own."

"*Oh, I'm sure—*," began Tim and Uncle James, both together.

"And when he does," said Aunt Bridget, "or *she* does—because it's probably some poor thrifty woman, if I know the menfolk around here—when *she* goes to claim it there's to be no taking any reward. You understand, Tim? The act is its own reward, till you get to heaven."

"Yes, ma'am," said Tim.

"But of course if no one *does* reclaim it," said Uncle James, "inside three months, then the money's ours—er—his."

"Ours," said Tim. "I'll be sharing it, you know."

"Well, be that as it may," said Aunt Bridget, "let us pray that the poor soul gets to hear about it."

"Oh, sure!" said Uncle James.

"Sure!" said Timothy.

"In fact I'll make it in my way to spread the word," said Aunt Bridget.

"You do just that, my dear," said Uncle James.

And he gave Tim a gentle kick under the table that was meant for a wink and a slap on the back—as the boy knew from past experience. It meant, in plain English: "We've done it, boy! It's worked! It's worked!"

Unfortunately—like many another statement of that sort, uttered in even plainer English—this one turned out to be far more optimistic than circumstances warranted.

CHAPTER SIX

The Claim

NOBODY is perfect.

True, Aunt Bridget came pretty close to her own idea of perfection. She didn't drink anything stronger than tea—not even coffee. She didn't smoke, and that included never allowing other people's tobacco smoke to enter her nostrils, if she could possibly help it at all. She said her prayers every night, went to church twice on Sundays, and brushed her teeth three times a day. ("Cleanliness," she was often saying, "comes next to Godliness," and she always acted as if it came a very close second indeed, almost a photo finish.) Gambling of course was out completely—so completely that she would have been horrified if she'd ever caught anyone in the house playing cards for matches or pretzels, let alone money. But then she would never allow playing cards in the house anyway, simply because there were people in the world who *did* play for money. As for swearing, she did occasionally say things like "Heavens!" or "Heavens above!" or, when really mad, "Drat!"—but you could always tell from the look on her face immediately afterward that she felt very guilty about letting rip in this way. In fact she would usually go straight to the bathroom at such times, from behind the door of which might then be heard the vigorous scrubbing of teeth.

But there was one thing that ruined Aunt Bridget's record time and time again. There was one thing she couldn't resist—one vice, one sin, one weakness, one pleasure, whatever you like to call it—and that one thing was gossip. *She* called it a sin and it gave her conscience a lot of trouble. Uncle James and Tim knew this only too well, because when she was troubled in this way she became for a few days even more severe than usual about *their* sins and weaknesses. Yet they had to admit she was honest. She never tried to talk herself into thinking that gossip was an innocent harmless pastime, or pretend that she never had slipped.

There were times, however, when she came near to finding an excuse for gossiping. If, for example, one of her neighbors was sick and had to stay in bed, Aunt Bridget would spend hours sitting at the invalid's side, telling her all the local news. "It does the poor soul a world of good," she would explain to Uncle James, on returning—after which the man would wink slyly at his nephew as if to say, "Yes, and it does *her* a world of good too, if you ask me!" Then again, if ever a policeman or detective came around making inquiries about some crime or accident in the neighborhood, Aunt Bridget would be sure to seize the opportunity to have a good old gossip with *him*, in the interests of responsible citizenship.

That then was the reason she'd been so specially keen to offer to spread the news about the sock and its contents. It gave her a glorious chance to go around gossiping with friends and acquaintances on the juicy subject of who the secret miser of the district might be, which led on so naturally to her all-time favorite topic of who were the district's obvious spendthrifts and ne'er-do-wells.

At first, Uncle James and Tim were amused by this.

"It's almost worth a thousand bucks to see how happy the telling of the finding of it is making her," said Uncle James, the following morning.

But by late afternoon he was not so sure.

"I'll be damned, my boy, if your aunt hasn't been blabbering about it in every store and supermarket for

twenty blocks in all directions," he announced. "Because
that's where they've been coming from."

"Who?" asked Tim.

"All day. Pouring into the station house."

"Who? Who?"

"Folks who claim the money to be theirs. Patrolman
Rafferty's just been telling me about it. And judging from
what he says, I'd have said some of them stores she's been
yacking in must have been liquor stores, if I didn't know
her better. . . . But that's just it. She only has to tell one
person in one supermarket and that one'll spread it to fifty
more, all over the neighborhood.

"But they won't be able to prove it's theirs, any of
them . . . er, *will* they, Uncle?" asked Tim, beginning to
feel uneasy.

Uncle James gave a short little laugh and clapped him
on the shoulder.

"Of course not! How can they? Why, they can't even
guess at the numbers of those bills, though some of 'em
have been having a try, according to Rafferty. That was
why I asked for a mixture of used ones, my boy. All the
numbers in the world. And by making it clear you found
them *near* a garbage can—not *in* one—but in the public
gutter—neither the sanitation department nor the owner
of the can will be able to claim the money instead of
us. Rafferty thought he had me there, till I pointed it
out. . . ."

"And there really have been so many people, though?
Already?"

"Sure! A stream of 'em, says Rafferty. All day. In fact I
was thinking of taking a little stroll along there to see for
myself. Why don't you come with me? It'll pass half an
hour or so very nicely till your aunt gets home."

It could hardly have been called a "stream" of people
going up the broad stone steps of the station house and

through the arched doorway. And it was impossible to tell from over the street what everyone's business was. Some might have been going to report missing cars; others might have been plainclothes detectives. Yet it did seem pretty busy to Tim and his uncle, and the cop on duty at the steps was sweating as he tried to check up on those going in.

"Now *there's* one who's after the money, my boy," Uncle James would keep saying. "You can tell by the wild look in his eye."

Or: "She now—*she's* after a try for it. There's something about the way her elbows stick out."

Or: "There—see that one? He's the superintendent of the building near where you said you found it. *He's* not come to buy a ticket for the Police Ball, that's for sure!"

As they watched and wondered, Tim began to feel uneasy again. Suppose someone did have a guess at the numbers on some of the notes and was lucky? It could be enough to convince the police. And if all these people were coming in to claim it, and it had been as busy as this or even busier all day, wouldn't the officers on duty be only too glad to get rid of the money and get back to normal again?

Uncle James didn't appear to share these anxieties. He was positively enjoying himself, especially as he tried to read the faces of some of the people on the way out.

"*She* didn't take long," he would say. "I bet she's a regular. I bet she claims anything she gets wind of. I bet they just throw her out before she even gets to the desk."

Or: "Heh! heh! Here comes the superintendent guy. Don't he look mad?"

And he was just reassuring Tim—having caught the look on the boy's face—when it happened.

"Now there's absolutely nothing to fear, my boy, absolutely nothing," he was saying. "How *can* anybody prove the money's theirs when we know for a fact where it really came from? It stands to—"

"Hello there, James, me beauty! Make way for a feller who's just had a tremenjous weight lifted off of his mind!"

They turned to see the newcomer, who had just rounded the corner behind them. For a second or two Uncle James blinked, then he grinned and stuck out his hand.

"Cornelius!" he cried. "Cornelius Murphy! I didn't recognize you in them duds!"

Tim smiled and nodded his head. He too had been fooled for a moment.

Cornelius Murphy was well known to most people in the neighborhood—a grizzled little man who might have been five foot ten or even six feet if it hadn't been for the bowedest pair of legs in the whole of Manhattan. As it was, he measured only a little over five feet. In fact it really did look as if the great weight he'd said he'd had on his mind had left his legs permanently bowed like that—though they knew him better than to believe he'd ever worried about anything for longer than five minutes at a time.

Like Uncle James, he'd been born in Ireland and had come over as a young man. Like Uncle James he had been married to a woman with very strict views, especially on the behavior of husbands and other male relatives. But Mrs. Murphy had been dead these last twenty years and Cornelius had let himself go, with great cheerfulness, ever since—seldom taking a bath more than once a month, and changing his clothes only when the spirit moved him, which was even less frequently. Tim had never seen him before in anything but the same old green sport coat and a pair of blue-serge pants concertinaed around his legs—pants that had a wonderful selection of grease stains that sometimes looked quite beautiful and rainbowlike when caught in certain kinds of sunlight. This however was a rare sight, since Mr. Murphy usually kept well indoors during the hours of daylight, preferably in the nearby poolroom.

But today it was different. Cornelius Murphy was
wearing on those legs a pair of black and gray pin-striped
pants that looked almost snappy. There were, admittedly,
a few small stains here and there, and one or two tiny
holes that mocked the reek of mothballs that was disturbed every time he rocked from one foot to the other.
There were similar stains and holes on and in the smooth
black coat he was wearing—and a similar reek when he
jerked an arm to free his fingers from the overlong sleeve.
But all in all he looked a new man, a much cleaner and
smarter man, and this impression was topped off by the
little black derby hat he'd dug up from somewhere to
replace the greasy old cap he usually wore, its bent peak
drooping over one ear.

"These," said Cornelius, "is the duds I buried poor
dear Mary in." He rubbed a gnarled and freckled and
moderately clean hand across his cheeks under the eyes,
but otherwise kept up the broad grin he'd started out
with. "Poor Mary! It was she who taught me the habit of
thrift which is making this such a great day for the
Murphys."

"Ho! ho!" cried Uncle James, giving Tim a nudge. "So
you're having a try for the money yourself, are ye?"

Mr. Murphy sniffed and cocked a pale blue eye up at
Uncle James.

"If it's the t'ousand bucks it took me the most of
twenty years to save, and which it nearly broke me poor
ould heart to lose the other day—yes. And what of it?"

"Argh, come on, Cornelius! You know you've never
saved a thousand *cents* in your whole life, never mind a
thousand dollars!"

Cornelius sniffed again, and swiveled the blue eye
down and across to Tim. "They tell me it was you who
found it, young feller?" he said, ignoring Uncle James.

Tim nodded, on guard.

"And they tell me you found it near the garbage cans

outside the building where I—as everybody knows except
the malicious and the envious—" up went the blue eye in
Uncle James's direction for a moment "—in which I happen to live and have lived for thirty-odd years."

"Ah, but come on now, Cornelius, that's no proof!"
said Uncle James, still grinning, still enjoying himself.

"No? . . . *No?*" Mr. Murphy looked as if he were
about to spring from those coiled-up legs of his and hit
Uncle James right on the nose. Then he too grinned,
allowing his tongue to loll out at the side of his mouth and
take a little strength from the sun, ready for what he was
about to get it to say. "Well now, listen. . . . All right.
. . . You have your little joke, Jim O'Connell—you're no
better nor worse than the others I been talking to. But me,
I have better proof than the exact spot where this good
honest lad here found it. Oh, yes!"

"You have the numbers, I suppose?" said Uncle James,
with a faint jeer in his voice and a nudge for Tim.

This time the fierce blue stare settled just above Uncle
James's belt buckle, as if the old man were thinking of
striking first there. Then once again it swiveled across to
Tim and became mellow.

"How does it feel to be blessed with a fool for a uncle,
lad?" he sighed. "Of *course* I can't remember the numbers!
But listen, lad, tell me this. What was it you found the
money *in,* eh?"

"A—a sock."

"So what?" laughed Uncle James. "Everybody knows
that!"

"And what sort of a sock was this, young feller? Eh?"

"Well . . . I . . . "

"You can tell him, boy," said Uncle James. "Everybody
knows that too. It'll make no difference."

"It was, was it not, a purple sock?" went on the old
man, speaking softly and slowly, but with great clarity.
"And it had yeller stripes, running crisscross, had it not?"

As Tim nodded, suddenly feeling uneasier than ever, Uncle James laughed again.

"Everybody knows *that,* too—after Bridget went a-blabbering it about the whole island. *That'*ll not get you past first base, old friend!"

"Maybe not!" growled Cornelius, suddenly clapping a hand on Tim's shoulder and making him jump. "But just look at this!"

Whereupon, leaning on Tim, he lifted a leg.

They stared, as it came up in a broad pin-striped arc. They stared as the concertinaed cloth began to stretch and reveal, at the cuff, a bright patch of yellow . . .

And purple.

"It—it's the same sock!" cried Tim. "Where—?"

"Not the *same,*" said the old man, still waving the leg in the sunlight, and gazing with deep admiration at the sock. "Not exactly. But the twin to it. . . . I was saving this one for me second thousand, starting a week on Wednesday. But me fool of a daughter started in spring-cleaning while me back was turned and threw the other out, money and all, with a lot of other stuff she chose to call junk. Heh! heh! You should have seen *her* face when she found out!"

By now Uncle James had recovered a little.

"Well what's on your other foot, then? There's probably hunrets of pairs like that."

Cornelius hopped on to his purple-and-yellow foot, clamped a hand on Timothy's shoulder again, swung up the other leg, and revealed an old green sock.

"One of my lucky pair," he said, putting the leg down again.

"Lucky pair!" Uncle James was laughing once more, not as loudly, but with a little more confidence than he'd been showing in these last few moments. "You'll need all the luck you can get to prove that *that* sock really is the twin of that one in there."

Again the hand clamped down on Tim's shoulder. But
this time it was to give Mr. Murphy his balance while he
drew off his shoe.

Then: "What about this, then? See *this?*"

He wriggled the foot in front of them, drawing attention to the clumsy green patch at the toe.

"I darned that meself. I darned it with the green wool
that was some old knitting wool I found amongst poor
Mary's belongings after she passed over. I darn everything
with this, even though it's not regular darning wool. Me
daughter's always yacking at me about it. But now she's
gonna wish she hadn't. Because, James O'Connell, if that
sock in the station house yonder is darned the same way—
with the same wrong wool—which it is—my claim is
proved."

Out came his tongue again as he slipped the shoe back
on, grinning from one to the other.

"And now, if you'll step aside, gintlemen, I'll be over to
take back what is rightfully mine. . . ."

That evening, Aunt Bridget had a radiant smile on her
face even before she'd checked on the shoe rack and the
other things.

"Have you heard the good news?" she said. "The
owner of the money has been found!"

Uncle James nodded glumly.

"We heard," he sighed.

"Yes," murmured Tim, studying the neat gray darning
patches in his own socks. "We already heard."

"Well put your slippers on and don't look so miserable," said his aunt. "And James—you've gotten the rug
creased up. Just straighten it out."

As they wearily obeyed her and she began setting her
things down on the chair by the door, she relaxed again—
even to the extent of humming a little tune. It was a hymn
tune, yes, and not a very sprightly one at that, but it was a

sign that Aunt Bridget had reached the peak of happiness for a while.

"You'll have heard who it was, then?" she said, coming around to sit with them.

"Oh, sure!" said Tim.

"Yes, we've heard," said Uncle James.

"Well I don't know which makes me happier," said Aunt Bridget. "Him finding his money again or me finding out that he isn't the little drunken waster I'd taken him to be."

Uncle James cocked an eye at her.

"You've found *that* out also, have you? . . . Well I must say it's news to me."

"And me," said Tim.

"What's the matter with you both? Are you so steeped in wrong ways you can't rejoice at such a blessing?"

Uncle James cleared his throat.

"We *are* talking about the same person, are we? We are talking about that little bandy-legged rat-faced—"

"James! If you go on using such language I shall walk straight out of this house and you'll have your own suppers to get. . . . Yes, I do mean Mr. Cornelius Murphy."

Uncle James sniffed.

"Hah! . . . So it's Mister now, is it? The other day it was 'That Dirty Little Waster' if I remember aright. 'That Dirty Little Waster Cornelius Murphy' was the exact words."

"I know, I know. And shame on me for being so uncharitable. But I didn't know then what a thrifty soul he was. Why, he must have gone without meal after meal, every week, to save that amount from the money *he* has coming in."

"Hmmph! He didn't seem to go without drink after drink very often."

"But he did save on soap, Uncle," said Tim bitterly.

"Now that's enough!" snapped his aunt. "I really don't know what's come over you both. Why, last week you were defending the poor little man when I was saying some hard things about him in the error of my thinking!"

"Yeah. Last week. That was last week."

"James O'Connell, I do believe you're jealous of him. Shame on you! If you're so envious, why don't *you* show a little more thrift and save up a thousand dollars?"

Uncle James looked ready to explode. With an obvious effort, he shut his eyes and turned his head.

"And you, Timothy O'Connell—I'm beginning to suspect you're *sorry* the poor man got his money back. I'm beginning to suspect you're wishing he'd never got to hear about it, so you could claim the lot!"

Tim hung his head. It might have looked like shame, but—as with Uncle James—it was fury.

"And one other thing," said Aunt Bridget, probably thinking she'd got him on the run. "I hope you minded what I said and refused the reward."

Uncle James made a choking noise and turned his head further away. His knuckles went white as he gripped the arms of the chair. He shot out a foot in a kick of anguish. Luckily nothing got in the way of it.

Aunt Bridget was watching Tim. "Well, *did* you refuse the reward?"

Somehow Tim managed to get the words out. "He—he didn't offer one."

Even Aunt Bridget looked a little shocked at that. But she rallied quickly. "Oh, well. . . ."

It was more than the boy could stand. Normally quiet and polite, it didn't mean he hadn't some of the spirit of his birthplace lurking inside him. Suddenly the old kings and warriors of Ireland who'd been slumbering there stirred, blinked, looked around, listened, grew angry—and leaped up.

"He didn't offer a reward," cried the boy, "because he's a lousy, mean, dirty, double-crossing, lying little crook! Why, it wasn't even his money, not a single cent of it, *and* he knows it! The sock, oh sure, the sock might have been his, and that's all he should have gotten, and welcome. But the money isn't his and never was and I hope the devil takes him and every lousy dollar of it. . . ."

"Steady, boy, steady!" Uncle James was murmuring, his mouth and eyes looking horrified but his ears having the time of their lives.

Aunt Bridget had gone all cold and straight.

"Timothy O'Connell!" she finally gasped. "I never knew you had such uncharitable thoughts inside you. Or such evil words. Go straight to your room, right now, and don't come out till you've put your soul to rights. Go on!"

Tim went. He didn't care. It was worth it. But it did make him wonder if they ever *would* be able to enjoy the money that was rightfully theirs. It did make him wonder if they wouldn't have been better off without it at all, if they'd never even won it in the first place.

But that was before Uncle James had crept in with a pocketful of cookies and a hissed warning to mind the crumbs, about an hour later, while Aunt Bridget was in the bathroom.

"Don't be downhearted, my boy," he whispered, as he tiptoed back to the door. "I just had me a great idea—a real winner. It simply can't go wrong, this one. You'll see."

CHAPTER SEVEN

The Eccentric Millionaire

"You got it, Uncle?"

It was the morning after Cornelius Murphy had ruined their plan. Aunt Bridget had gone off to work and Uncle James—after pretending to go off to *his* work—had returned, carrying a small but bulky brown-paper sack.

He patted the sack now and grinned.

"It's all here, boy!"

"Do you mind if I see it?"

"Aw, it's just the same as the other lot. Used notes again."

Uncle James was beginning to look hunted. He clutched tighter at the sack and rolled an uneasy eye in the direction of the door.

"Go on, Uncle. Please! Just a quick peek."

"It's only money, my boy. Bills." Uncle James sighed. "That's one thing I'm learning fast. Money's only interesting when you can buy things with it. Money itself— well—I just can't understand them misers hoarding it all up just so's they can count it every night. *You're* not getting like that, are ye, Tim?"

"No! 'Course not! But it might make me feel better, just seeing it, after what happened to the last thousand."

"Go on, then," Uncle James thrust out the sack and opened the top, "just a quick look. . . . Okay?"

Tim nodded. He smiled. Just as he'd hoped, the sight of those wads of green bills, nestling in the shade, made him feel happier. He even began to feel happier about old Cornelius Murphy himself—almost glad to have been partly responsible for bringing the old rogue such a magnificent windfall.

"Right," said Uncle James, carefully folding up the top of the sack and holding it tight and snug in the crook of his arm. "Let's get moving. We've got to do this thing properly, over in the park, before it gets too busy there."

"You sure I can't just *say* about the park?"

"No, you *cannot*. We got to keep you in the clear with the Good Lord up above, boy, and this way you won't have to tell any fibs. Besides," Uncle James added, as they stepped out into the street, "it'll help to give weight to your story."

And that is how there came to be enacted in the little park not far from their home a very strange scene. It was still quite early and not many people were around to see it. Terry Noone and a few of the other kids were there, but they were too busy playing ball, up on the courts behind the high wire fence, to notice Tim and his uncle as they entered. And even the people who did witness the performance—mainly elderly men and women settling down to their morning papers or chats under the trees— even these people merely glanced across and thought nothing of it.

For one thing, it looked like just another everyday little incident, with a man handing a boy a package of sandwiches, or bagels, or cookies. And for another thing, nobody was near enough to hear exactly what the two were saying. Naturally, had they known that that paper sack was full of assorted ten- and twenty-dollar bills, to the total of one thousand dollars, they might have got to their feet and edged closer. And had they done *that*—had they edged closer—they might have overheard the whole weird conversation. . . .

"Oh, good morning, my boy! You look a nice bright lad. I bet your name's Timothy, isn't it?"

"Sure it is, Uncle! You know very well—"

"Whisht! Whisht! Forget I'm your uncle, now will *you? Let's start over again.* . . . Ah, good morning, my boy! You look a nice bright lad. I bet your name's Timothy, isn't it?"

"Er—yes, sir—it is. It—"

"I thought it was, I thought it was. Well now, listen, my boy. I am an eccentric millionaire and I once had a nephew the true spittin' image of yourself. He was called Tim also, poor boy."

"What—what happened to him, Unc— er—sir?"

"He died of eating crackers in bed, to tell you the full truth of it. Choked on a crumb, poor boy, and him saying his prayers an' all. . . . *Stop laughing, will yez? You got to get this story straight.* . . . Yes. He died in the flower of his boyhood. And ever since then I swore I would never rest till I found a lad like Tim, and *called* Tim, to give the money to. Take it, my boy. There's a whole thousand dollars in there. A present from an eccentric millionaire. Tell them that. Be sure to. If anybody asks. *And you can count on it she will.* Got it? A present from an eccentric millionaire."

"A present from a—an—"

"Eccentric. It means a bit crazy but well-to-do."

"A present from an eccentric millionaire."

"That's me boy. *Now ask me my name.*"

"Er—but I know it, Uncle."

"Whisht, will *ya? We're still acting it out, boy. Forget I'm your uncle. I am an eccentric millionaire and I've just given you this dough. Now c'm on, c'm on. Ask me my name."*

Tim asked.

Uncle James took a step back and onto the circular stone plinth that stood in the center of the courtyard type of area where they'd been talking. Usually the plinth was used by dogs or kids in their chasing games. Sometimes it was used by grown-ups who wished to make speeches in the evenings when the cops weren't around. Now it was being used as a kind of stage, as Uncle James warmed to his part.

"Ah," he said, in a low but sonorous and very dramatic voice, "do not ask me that, my boy! Do not ask of me my name. I—"

"But you just told me to!"

"*That was* me, *your uncle, telling you to ask. Now I'm being* him, *the eccentric millionaire again. . . . Just hold your tongue and listen or we'll be here all day. . . .*" Uncle James then put on his mysterious look and swiveled his eyes this way and that and bent his head to one side and put out a hand as if warding somebody off. "No, my boy," he went on, in the deep sad voice. "Do not ask my name of me. When us eccentric millionaires give things away like this we *never* tell our name. It's a rule. The word would get around, you see, and we'd be pestered with bums and panhandlers and telephone calls and begging letters and it would spoil all the fun. There's many an eccentric millionaire who's stopped doing this sort of thing, just because he was fool enough to give his name away along with a parcel of dough. So just take the money, lad, and enjoy it, and buy things with it on the way home."

Tim's eyes widened.

"You mean that, Unc— *sir?*"

"I do indeed. The thought just struck me and it must have been an angel sent it, it's so good. You buy things with that money on the way home. Whatever you fancy. For you and your loved ones. Just in case any of those loved ones gets any crazy idea into her head about making you hand over the dough to the police or something. Okay?"

"*Okay!*" Tim said, as delighted as his uncle at this new idea.

"And it was given you by an eccentric millionaire. Got it?"

"*Got* it!"

"Good!" Uncle James became himself again. There was a sparkle in his eyes as he tugged at his hat brim and stepped off the plinth. "So now let's go and do what the man said."

When Aunt Bridget opened the door of the apartment that afternoon she could hardly believe her eyes. She blinked. She dropped her pocketbook. She went white. She gasped. She turned to go, as if hardly able to believe this was where she lived, the place she had left so neat and clean but very poor and bare-looking, earlier in the day.

It was the sight of the two grinning faces that helped to reassure her a little.

"What—what's happened?" she managed to gasp out at last.

There was good cause for her amazement. The little room that usually saw one thin bunch of flowers about three times a year was now glowing and bristling and trumpeting with color in every corner: with carnations, with roses, with asters, with gladiolus, all in fat clusters, and in vases of crystal and bronze that she'd never set eyes on before.

And that was just a beginning.

On the chair by the door, on which she was in the habit of putting her pocketbook and packages, there lay a box, with the lid temptingly drawn to one side to reveal a brand-new vibromassager. It was of the kind that one of her richest employers had, and occasionally allowed her to use to ease the arthritis in her shoulders, and many had been the times that Aunt Bridget had confessed to her

husband and Tim that "The one luxury in all the world I'd
like would be one of those massaging machines like Mrs.
Van Elst's. It does do the shoulder good."

But she had scarcely had time to take in exactly what
it was when her eyes were drawn to the furry coat that
hung over the chairback. It was brand new. The label and
tickets were dangling from a string.

She turned to her husband to say something and then
stopped—her jaws open—as she noticed the gleaming
new bicycle propped against the wall just behind the
man. And when she turned to Tim she had another shock,
this time to notice that the triangle of white by his chair
wasn't a corner of the tablecloth at all, but the sail of a
huge model yacht at his feet.

And anyway—she must have thought—what was the
table doing ready laid at this time? And with the best
Sunday tablecloth, too? Which, in turn, made her take
another closer look at the table itself, and nearly swoon to
realize that on it, in the center, was a fat brown cold roast
duck, garnished with orange slices and greenery; and a
great bowl of fruit, peaches and grapes and a pineapple,
the sort of fruit that rarely graced *that* table, and then only
separately, never all at once; and around the edges of the
table were glass cups on stems, filled with plump pink
shrimps and more green stuff; and next to them were
glasses of water, crystal glasses such as Mrs. Van Elst
always warned her to handle with extra care; and there—
behind a bowl of carnations—what was that but a cake, a
delicious-looking cake with five layers?

"*Oh!*"

She gave a little start and no wonder, for from the
flowered chair had come a sudden unholy squealing and
pealing—and when she turned she gave nearly as big a
start to see that it was a piano accordion that her husband
was fumbling with, his own smile nearly as wide and

gappy as the keyboard along which he was running his fingers.

"And lookit, Aunt Bridget!" cried Tim, running to the sideboard and lifting something up. "This is for you, too. A radio set that wakes you up with music and makes tea or coffee."

"But—I—it—"

"Let me just point out whose is what, my dear," said Uncle James. "Just sit yourself down while I tell you. . . . This here . . ." he gave the accordion another pummeling "this here's mine—what I've always wanted and which I can learn to play in no time. Hymns, you understand. I'll learn a few of them, also. For the boy, the bicycle and the boat there—and let me say right now they was the last of the things he thought of getting."

"*He?* Timothy? He—"

"The radio set that makes tea is for you. So is the massage machine. So is the coat. It ain't real fur, but it's guaranteed to keep you a sight warmer this coming winter than that old blue thing you came near to catching pneumonia in last winter. The meal of course is for us all—we had it specially brought in, ready cooked. Same with the flowers. I mean they're for us all to enjoy too. But the dishes and the glassware and the vases I see you got your eye on—those are what Tim bought for the house, bought and paid for with—"

"*What?* With *what?*"

Aunt Bridget was looking almost panic-stricken as she glanced from face to face.

"Er—well—you'd better explain, Tim."

Tim wasn't quite sure how to begin. Then he remembered something.

"Look, Aunt Bridget!" he cried, lifting up his feet. "Moccasins. Real Indian moccasins. Made on a real Indian reservation. I got us a pair each."

Aunt Bridget didn't shift her now steely steady gaze from his face.

"Never mind about those," she said. "Where did the money come from? If you found a credit card like young Greg Schultz and went buying things before you turned it in—"

"No, no, *no,* my dear! Tim wouldn't do anything like *that!* Just hear the lad out and you'll see. . . . Go on, Tim. Tell her from the beginning. In the park. You were in the park . . ."

So, stumbling a little at first but soon picking up strength and confidence, Tim told her about how a man had given him the package, and why, and everything (or almost everything) that was said. The fact that he didn't bother to tell her the man had been his uncle made it all the easier. That way he didn't have to tell even a tiny fib. And what helped all the more was the way his aunt drank it all in. Only twice did she interrupt him. The first time was to inquire if he'd thought to ask the man's name and address, whereupon Tim simply gave her the answer the "eccentric millionaire" had given him. And the second time was to ask what the man looked like, which Tim answered simply and truthfully enough with a description of his Uncle James.

She didn't even spot the similarity, so far from her mind was the possibility that her husband could be going around giving away obviously real money in such huge quantities.

"We still have quite a bit of it left," said Tim, reaching down and picking up the now crumpled and much less bulky paper sack.

She took it off him in silence and peered inside. Then she gave a shudder and folded over the top as if she'd spied a nest of young rats in there.

"The poor creature!" she said. "The poor crazed creature!"

The Eccentric Millionaire

"Well, I wouldn't exactly say *poor*, my dear," murmured Uncle James, beginning to look a little less cheerful.

"The poor, poor soul!" sighed Aunt Bridget, as if she'd not even heard her husband. "And to think it might have been the loss of that little boy nephew of his that unhinged him! That—that poor little Timothy!"

There was a sob in her voice as she said this. Two fat tears began to roll down two thin cheeks.

Tim gave his uncle an accusing look. He'd felt all along that the man had tended to overdo things with his playacting in the park.

"Well, of course," said Aunt Bridget, getting up and putting the paper sack on the table, "we can't take advantage of him like this. We must give it all back. Everything. Every single thing. The rest of the money and everything you bought."

"But, Aunt Bridget, he *told* me—"

"I know. I know, Tim. I'm not really blaming you. I'm not even blaming your uncle for helping you to spend it—for it's only the brains of a boy he's got also. But you just simply can't go around taking money from crazy people, even when they give it you freely."

"Ah, yes! But you see, my dear, he wouldn't give his name, let alone his address. How *can* we give it back?"

Aunt Bridget nodded sadly. She dried her cheeks, sniffing. Then she said, "That's what's been worrying me. But I think I know now what the Good Lord in heaven would have us do. I think I hear the message. . . . There is always the church to pass things like this on to the truly needy. Timothy, get your shoes on and brush your hair. You as well. We're taking this lot across right away."

"But—the food—the flowers—surely—?"

"Them we can take to the hospital. It's only just around the corner, and there's many a poor soul in there whose eyes'll brighten when they see what we have for them here."

As they made their first journey, burdened with the packed and parceled treasures, Uncle James managed to whisper a few words to Tim.

"That's done it then!" he growled. "That has done it, my boy. This is the last straw." He jerked the parcels in his arms into a more comfortable position and, so doing, caused the accordion at the bottom to give a faint, unearthly groan. "Tomorrow we leave. Tomorrow we make arrangements to move out—just me and you."

The parcel's groan had already startled the boy. But the man's last words made him go quite cold.

Did his uncle really mean it?

"And this time I mean it, my boy!" muttered the man, as if he'd read Tim's horrified thoughts.

CHAPTER EIGHT

The New Life

"You DIDN'T really mean it, did you, Uncle?"

"Oh yes I did!"

It wasn't until late the following morning that Tim had a chance to question his uncle about what he had said on the subject of leaving. They'd all been so busy the night before—handing over the gifts and the remaining money, and then trying to eat a meal of tuna fish, lettuce and tomatoes after seeing the duck and the other delicacies laid out on the same table—that there'd been no opportunity for a private chat. What had made it worse was the fact that Uncle James hadn't even tried to slip into Tim's room on the pretext of saying good night in order to carry on the conversation in quick whispers, as he often did; and Tim had lain awake for hours, waiting and worrying in vain. Then, that morning, Uncle James had left the apartment even earlier than Aunt Bridget. He had gobbled his breakfast, listened in silence to his wife's usual lecture on the damage such gobbling did to one's insides, then had put on his shoes and hat, muttering something about "a very special job that's just got to be completed this day."

Now he was back, just after eleven thirty, looking strangely flushed—tight-lipped and serious—but with a happy gleam in his eyes.

"We *can't* leave her, Uncle! You said yourself when we won the money. You said yourself that we couldn't just go off and leave Aunt Bridget. I mean I *know* it's tough, not being able to spend our money in the open and all, but it's even tougher on her."

"Oh?" Uncle James raised his eyebrows and looked down at Tim curiously. "And how d'you figure *that* out, my boy?"

"Well, last night for example. Did you see how she looked when she first saw that massage-machine thing? She looked like she could have jumped up and down, clapping her hands."

"Your aunt do such a thing as that? You're joking, boy!"

"Well, you know what I mean. For one little minute she was real happy. Then did you notice the way she looked when she handed it over. It really hurt her to part with it. There were tears in her eyes, Uncle. I saw them."

"My own eyes was too brimming over at the thought of parting with the accordion to notice what hers were doing. But go on. . . ."

"Well, it did really hurt her. But she went through with it. It wasn't so bad for us. *We* knew there was *lots* more money where that thousand dollars had come from. She didn't. As far as she knew, that was the last chance she'd ever get to have one of those machines."

"Yeah? And what makes you think we'll be getting another chance to buy ourselves accordions and bicycles and whatnot—money or no money?" But Uncle James was grinning now. He slapped Tim on the shoulder. "I know what you mean though, my boy. Sourpuss or no sourpuss, your aunt's an angel at heart—and if only we could hit on a way of getting her to accept the money everything would be fine. Why, if her shoulders didn't ache so much she might relax enough to take a little pleasure in life. Same with if she didn't work so hard and get herself so tired. It would make a new woman of her. But the trick is to get her *started*—and so far my old head's not come up with anything."

Tim felt better.

"So it was just a bit of temper then?"

"What was just a bit of temper?"

"You saying last night about us moving out and leaving her."

Uncle James was still smiling. But he was also shaking his head. "Not a bit of it, my boy. I was never so determined in my life. And this morning I've been making all the arrangements." He sighed happily. "It's amazing how quick you can get things done when you have the money."

"But—"

"These," said Uncle James, producing a pair of small gold-colored keys and swinging them slowly in front of Tim's nose, "these is the keys to the New Life, my boy, the Sweet Life, the Good Life—the new life for me and you. . . . And of course for your aunt, soon as we think of a way to get her to see sense."

Tim moved nearer his uncle, seeking to detect a whiff of strong drink. He smelled nothing but a kind of rich perfume that must still have been clinging to the keys.

"These," continued Uncle James, "is the keys to our new apartment. If we like it when we see it. Just off Fifth Avenue, as near the Central Park Zoo as possible. Furnished in the best style, with everything you could wish for—including color television, grand pianner, cocktail bar, refrigerator, two bathrooms, air-conditioning, room service if you want it—the whole bit. I thought maybe you'd like to come along there with me now and give it the once-over."

"Near Fifth Avenue?"

"We can afford it."

"Near the zoo?"

"A weakness of mine. One which I'm hoping you will be sharing with me. Watching the animals of the jungle and marveling at them. One of the joys of boyhood I missed out on—my mother being a bit too much like your

aunt for comfort. Then there's the model-sailboat pool—
another little weakness of mine. . . . What?"

Tim was shaking his head.

"It's no use, Uncle. She wouldn't come with us. Not
even if we said we were never coming back here. Not
when she heard where the money had come from."

"Who said anything about never coming back here,
boy? We'll be back every night. Listen. . . . This is the
plan. . . . Every morning, I'll be setting off in my working clothes as usual. But instead of going to work—which
I'm through with, anyways, or sneaking back here as soon
as your aunt's gone, which is what I've been doing this
last day or two—why, I'll be going around to our Fifth
Avenue apartment."

"Yes, but—"

"Whisht, while I put you in the picture. . . . I'll be
turning up there, changing my clothes—I've already
ordered five new outfits from Brooks Brothers—taking a
little light refreshment on the balcony, then sallying
forth into the pleasure groves of Central Park, starting
with the zoo. . . . You, of course, will be with me—
during the vacation at least. In fact I've taken the liberty
of ordering a couple of new outfits for you as well."

"But—for *me?* What sort? Flare-bottomed levis? Did
you remember—? Oh, but listen, what about Aunt
Bridget?"

"Of course I remembered the flare-bottoms, lad. . . .
As to your Aunt Bridget, she need never know. Because,
just like Cinderella—only on the day shift—at the stroke
of five P.M. we'll be changing back into our everyday duds
and coming back here."

Tim's eyes were wide and shining now.

"Gee, Uncle!" he cried. "You really do have some good
ideas!" Then his face clouded a little. "But there's still
Aunt Bridget. What about getting *her* to come too? For
good?"

Uncle James nodded.

"That we will be working on, my boy. Just as we've been doing ever since we won the money. But we might as well be doing it in comfort and style. There's no telling what a little enjoyment and luxury might do to get the old brain working smoothly. . . . But come on. We're wasting time. We've got to see if the rugs is thick enough and the view is all that the guy at the real-estate office said it was. . . ."

It wasn't often that Tim passed through the streets at the side of Fifth Avenue. When he did, it was usually while he was on his way to Central Park—and then he'd always been too busy thinking about what he was going to do in the park to pay much attention to his surroundings on the way there.

Now that there was the prospect of living in such an area, however, it was different. He found himself noticing every detail, as he padded along at the side of his uncle. He noticed, for instance, that here *all* the apartment buildings had long canopies between the entrances and the curb—to ensure that not one drop of rain should fall on any resident or visitor on the way to his car or taxi. He noticed too that every doorman in these parts wore a complete uniform—hat, coat, pants and sometimes gloves —all in a crisp lightweight material that kept them cool as well as smart, as they darted out to open the doors of those cars or taxis. As for the cars themselves—Tim thought he'd never seen so many Cadillacs and Lincolns; so many Eldorados and Fleetwoods; so many Mercedes and Bentleys; all in one area, all in such sparkling condition. ("We'll be getting something of the kind ourselves, my boy," murmured Uncle James, seeing him drag his feet and stare. "Just you wait!")

Then there were the little things—the not so obvious things—that Tim noticed too. The absence of ugly iron fire escapes up the fronts of the buildings. (But what happens when there *is* a fire? he couldn't help wondering.) And the shortage of front stoops. (But where do the people sit, evenings? And what do kids bounce their balls off?)What stoops there were were usually barred off from the sidewalks by heavy black railings, and fancy iron gates that locked, and the steps had so many tubs of plants or bits of statues on them that there was hardly room for one person to sit on them, let alone a whole family at a time, with their friends and relations.

It was all very clean, of course. He'd expected that. There were no old wrappers, empty Coke cans, broken bottles strewn about. There weren't even any garbage cans in view, either. But what surprised him was the fact that everything paintable—but everything—seemed to have been given a new coat that very morning. Doors, window frames, railings, even the grilles at the side of the walls or around the bases of the beautifully trimmed trees at the edge of the sidewalks. With every pace he walked it made Tim wonder who saw to all this painting and sweeping and trimming and polishing, for, apart from the doormen—and somehow, in all their finery, they didn't seem to count—there wasn't a workman in sight.

Unless . . .

Suddenly Tim began to feel a little uncomfortable.

Unless—he reminded himself—you counted Uncle James, still in his working clothes: drill pants, check shirt, denim coat, floppy hat.

"Hey, Uncle," he began, "are you sure—?" He was going to say, "Are you sure the doorman'll let us in, looking the way we do?" when Uncle James cut him short.

"This," he said, putting a hand on the boy's shoulder and looking at a small card he'd had stuck in his hatband, "is it."

And, without a second glance at the sign with an

arrow pointing to the tradesmen's entrance, he went
straight up to the doorman.

The man was the finest of all the fine specimens Tim
had seen that morning. He was tall and very fair and wore
a spotless uniform the color of milky coffee. He also had
on a pair of glasses with thick horn rims that made him
look much more like a doctor than a doorman, to Tim's
way of thinking.

"Yes?" he said, in a voice as soft as butter—the sort of
voice that had never been ruined by the task of telling
kids, five times an hour, to clear off and play someplace
else. "Can I help you?"

Even Uncle James seemed a little put off now, under
that steady blue gaze from on high.

"Well—I—er—I've called to see about the apartment
on the twelfth floor, facing the park—12D, I think . . ."

As Uncle James stumbled along with his tale, Tim
began to feel wretched. It was all a mistake. Money or no
money, this was no place for them. Any second now, that
doorman was going to order them straight back on the
street, or call the cops, or—worse still—say something
about trying the tradesmen's entrance.

But Tim had a lot to learn about doormen in this part
of town. Doormen in this part of town—he had to learn—
were a lot different from the ones he knew. These were
the specialists, the stars, the cream of their profession.
And this one was at the very top of the league.

"Certainly, sir," he said. "I was told to expect you. You
will be Mr. O'Connell and this—" he bestowed on Tim a
warm, wide smile "—this will be your nephew Tim you
mentioned at the estate office. I'm Jenkins and I hope
you'll be pleased with what you see up there. Apart from
the penthouse it's certainly one of the finest apartments in
the whole building. . . ."

As they rode up in the elevator, listening to the soft

sweet music and marveling at the carpet and the paneling, Uncle James winked at Tim.

"That's what I call a very pleasant welcome, my boy. I think we're gonna like it here."

"Yes, Uncle. I was beginning to think—"

"What? He'd throw us out? Nonsense! It doesn't matter what you're wearing so long as you have the money. *Or* the way you talk. *Money* talks. . . ."

Then: "Correction," he said, as they stepped out into the wide quiet cool corridor, decorated with pictures and vases of flowers on small shiny tables every so often. "Money *sings*, my boy—sings sweet and low."

And, with a little jingle, he lifted the keys to the locks on the door marked 12D.

CHAPTER NINE

The New Apartment

UNCLE JAMES needn't have worried even a little bit about the rugs and the view. The rugs were thick and the view was wide. And when the thickness is of pure wool, soft and springy, and the width takes in a stretch of Manhattan that includes much of Central Park, there can be little room for complaint.

There was plenty of space for other things, though. The main room, with French windows leading straight on to the balcony, was large enough to have taken almost the whole of the O'Connells' usual apartment.

"Why!" cried Uncle James, as he looked it up and down and across. "Think of all the parties we could hold in here, boy! Come Christmas and with a bit of luck concerning your aunt, we could hold a grand reunion of the O'Connells in this very room. Just think of that! With a tree in the corner right there and the table along the side here and the rugs all pulled up for dancing and the pianner there all ready. . . . Ah, the pianner! Didn't I tell you it had a grand pianner?"

Reverently, Uncle James walked springing and sinking across the thick rug and stood over the instrument, running a finger gently across the polished wood lid.

"Who's bothered about an old piano accordion when there's one of these in the house?" he said, opening it up and playing softly and haltingly the first few bars of "Bryan O'Lynn."

But Tim was more interested in the television and

whether it really was a color set. Then, having satisfied himself that it was, he went exploring the other rooms, with his uncle wandering after him.

"Nicely sprung," said the man, sitting on one of the twin beds in the main bedroom.

"So's mine," said Tim, taking off his shoes and doing a flip on the bed in the next room.

Uncle James came over to the door and sighed.

"But of course we shan't be using them unless we *can* get your aunt to change her mind," he said. "And even if we do, I bet you any money she'll say her bed's *too* springy."

"Hey, but wouldn't she just love this kitchen!" cried Tim, pressing on, wanting to see everything all at once. "All the space, these counters, and—wow!—lookit the refrigerator! *Is* it a refrigerator?"

"It sure is, my boy," said Uncle James, opening the door. "And—hello—what have we here?"

The shelves were all clean and bare except one. On this one was a six-pack of cola and four tiny dark-green bottles with golden foil around their corks.

"If it isn't champagne!" said Uncle James. " 'With the compliments of the management,' " he added, reading from a typewritten card on the same shelf. " 'Please help yourself. Glasses in cupboard over stove.' "

"Well now," said Uncle James, reaching up as directed, "that's what I call very civil. That's what I call doing things in style. We'll accept their kind invitation, of course?"

"You bet!" said Tim. "I never had a glass of champagne in my life."

"Nor will you till you're old enough!" said Uncle James, sounding rather like his wife at that moment. "Old enough to appreciate it, I mean. Here." He handed the boy a beaker and pointed to the six-pack.

But he relented a little, after the cork had popped from the bottle he'd selected for himself and the frothy liquid gushed out.

"Just a sip," he said. "And never, *never* let your aunt get word of this, even if she does get to know about the apartment itself."

Tim sipped, then curled up his nose.

"Don't like it anyway," he said, pouring himself a beaker of Coke.

"A toast," said Uncle James. He clinked his glass against the boy's beaker. "To the new life!"

"And now another," said Uncle James, pouring himself some more champagne. "To absent friends!"

They clinked once more.

By the time Tim had gone through two of the cans and Uncle James the third of the small bottles, and they'd toasted the President of the United States, the real-estate company, Mr. Jenkins down below, the memory of Tim's father, mother and young sister, killed in a car accident, the success of the Mets and the cheek of Cornelius Murphy—they'd already made up their minds.

"We'll have it. I'll give them the word right away."

"It must cost a lot though," said Tim, still not quite able to believe it.

"A dollar or two," said Uncle James. "But worth every cent, I should say, even if we shan't be using it full time."

"One of the bedrooms, the big one, we can fix a Ping-Pong table in it."

"My boy, what an angel of an idea! That sip of champagne must have done you good. . . . The small bedroom we'll keep for a changing-room. Or for if I need a little shut-eye after lunch."

"But you do like the Ping-Pong idea? And you will play with me? I mean you won't always be sleeping or—or—well—maybe just sitting on the balcony?"

"Of course not, lad! What d'you think I am? An old invalid or cripple or somethin'? I'll give ye such a game of Ping-Pong it'll be youse who'll be going crawling away for a rest. And we'll get ourselves a pool table while we're at it. And—here—here's one I been storing up: How about a real big train set with tracks running all over the place, room to room, with tunnels and sidings and stations and bridges and whatnot?"

Just as Uncle James was getting into his stride on the subject, the apartment's three telephones rang.

"Whyn't you take the one in there and listen in?" said Uncle James. "I got a feeling it's something you'll be specially interested in."

By the time the boy had picked up the bedroom phone, Uncle James was already speaking.

"Have you now? I thought it might be that, but I have to hand it to you—you move fast."

"We try our best, sir."

"Now you're sure it's the one you showed me this morning?"

"The very same, sir, yes, of course."

"And the papers and everything's in order?"

"Everything, sir."

"Okay. We'll be right down."

On the way out, Uncle James refused to answer any of Tim's questions. Only in the elevator, when the boy asked him why he'd pressed the basement button instead of the one for the first floor, did Uncle James unbend a little.

"Why," he said, "but that's where the garages always are in these places, isn't it?"

"Yes, but—garage?"

"That's where he said he'd delivered it to, didn't he?"

"*It?* A—a *car?*"

"Yeah. Why not? I said we'd be getting one, didn't I? Well—"

The doors slid open. Tim stared around at the cars near the elevator, wondering.

Then a voice said, "Over here, sir, by the door,"—and Tim saw it: a deep rich glowing green in a shaft of sunlight—one of the longest, sleekest cars the boy had ever come across, even counting the ones he'd passed that morning.

Uncle James coughed hesitantly, as he watched Tim's face.

"It's only a Cadillac, I'm afraid."

"*Only?*"

"Yeah, well—as you know—I had my heart set on a Rolls but delivery might have been a bit delayed and the feller showed me this and I guess I just couldn't resist."

"Uncle, she's a beauty!"

"Isn't she now? Come on, let's get the keys off the man and see'f she behaves as nice as she looks. . . ."

CHAPTER TEN

Snags

FROM THAT DAY ON, anyone keeping a close watch on that apartment building would have noticed a very strange procedure. They would have seen, in the mornings, shortly after eight o'clock, a rather shabby-looking workman and boy enter the building. Then—anything from an hour to ninety minutes later—the watcher would have seen the same pair emerge completely transformed.

In the late afternoon the same thing would happen in reverse. The transformed man and boy would enter the apartment building—laden with packages perhaps—and, half an hour later, moving a lot more slowly and less jauntily than at any other time of the day, out would come the shabby workman and the rather poorly dressed boy.

What the observer would not be able to guess from his notes would be the reason for the longer delay between appearances in the mornings than in the afternoons—though if he'd inquired of the doorman, Mr. Jenkins, he just might have been given the answer in one word.

"Breakfast," Mr. Jenkins might have said.

And, having said his one word, the doorman might have added a few more by way of explanation.

"It's the gentleman. He just goes mad over breakfasts. He sends down for breakfast every morning, as soon as he and the boy have changed, and you'd never believe the things he orders. At first it was wild—really wild—caviar and toast followed by the best fillet steak and topped off with ice cream. Things like that. Now it's settling down to something a little plainer. You know—like Irish bacon, specially flown in, and deviled kidneys, and new-laid eggs direct from a farm upstate, and Olde Englishe Marmalade. But still the ice cream. Soft ice cream. I think that's for the boy. Ice cream for breakfast!"

Regarding the transformation in appearances, an observer would have been able to see for himself that while the boy's was fairly simple—changing one set of jeans for another with wider bottoms, and his plain shirt for one with crazy patterns on it of the kind likely to be frowned on by a strict aunt, say—the man's was always a major production.

Some days, for example, you'd have to look more than twice to make sure it was the same man and not some ex-Navy officer of rear-admiral rank or above. But under the smart white cap with the shiny black peak there was the same face that had been under the floppy old hat going in. And the body that was now tricked out in the dark blue blazer with brass buttons, the immaculate white drill slacks and the rope-soled sneakers, the massive gold wristwatch guaranteed to go forever under water, and the red silk cravat patterned with what looked like an exclusive yacht-club's crest—that was the body of the shabby workman all right. And what was he doing dressed like that? The answer lay in the huge shiny-hulled model sailing boat under the boy's arm, and the direction they were taking, almost at a trot, straight across Fifth Avenue and into Central Park.

On the days they motored out into the country the man would select something different. Sometimes he'd be wearing a large straw hat with a bright green-and-white silk band around it; sometimes it would be a tweedy Sherlock Holmes type hat, with gaily colored artificial flies stuck into it. Again he'd prefer a blazer to any other sort of coat for his country jaunts—but it would be striped

instead of plain blue, and the color of the stripes would vary from day to day. At other times, when they left on foot for the shops or the bank, the man would wear something very sober, almost severe—usually a suit in a dark gray or blue, but remarkably light in weight. On these occasions he wouldn't bother with a hat of any kind, and this would enable any observer to see what a magnificent wig that "poor shabby workman" had managed to get for himself: fairly thick and with long fluffy sideburns, in a distinguished shade of gray that merged into white at the edges.

Tim and Uncle James did lots of shopping in that first glorious week. Naturally, clothes were the things they went out for at first, mainly on account of Uncle James— but it never took him long to decide. If he couldn't make up his mind between two articles he'd simply buy them both and have done with it, and anyway they'd always end up in the toys-and-sports department. Model-railroad sets, three different sailing boats, flippers and snorkel equipment, a set of table-tennis equipment, a junior drum kit, an inflatable canoe, a massive box of Everyboy's Master Disguises: these were just a few of the items they bought in those early days of their new life. And in such places Uncle James didn't hurry it up to anything like the same extent as he did in the clothes stores.

"Are you sure you don't mind, Uncle?" Tim would sometimes say, as he leaned over a model-train layout, or pressed and pulled the controls of a car-race circuit, trying to make up his mind what to buy. (For Uncle James had decided, with a twinge of conscience and in the hope of having some excuse to offer if his wife ever did get to know, that he'd set Tim a weekly allowance for such purchases, with an upper limit of three hundred dollars.)

"Of course not, my boy," the man would reply. "Take all the time in the world. These is the joys of boyhood I never tasted even as a man, and I got years to catch up on. . . . Hey, will you excuse me a minute now while I go and have a look at the puppets over there?"

So they came and went and made their trips and sorties, and for about ten days it was like living in a wonderful dream.

Then things started going wrong.

It was nothing very serious at first. In fact as far as Tim could make out it was just a feeling. Every so often, when he and his uncle were in the middle of something— a trip, a game, a meal—there would come this faint feeling of wistfulness: about how good it would be, or how even better it would be, to have another kid or two along to share with.

True, at the very start, there was something a bit mean about it: a longing to have someone like Terry Noone on hand to marvel at their new life and feel envious. But soon it became more straightforward than that. It was simply a realization that:

> (A) to really enjoy most games you need at least one other kid; and
>
> (B) no matter how hard he tried or how much he enjoyed some of those games, Uncle James was no longer a youngster.

The Ping-Pong was a perfect example. Sure, Uncle James had a very cunning service. Sure, he could put lots of top spin on the ball—a top spin it must have taken years to perfect. But in the matter of quick rallies, or going chasing after the ball under furniture, or being able to play more than three games in a row without needing a half-hour rest, he was no substitute for someone like Terry.

It was the same at the model-sailboat lake. Uncle
James always started out in grand style, striding around
the edge, bellowing orders to an imaginary crew, startling
the mothers and nurses as he strode over the little kids
playing in his path, and generally behaving like an ener-
getic giant. But after two circuits he left it all to Tim.
Then it was Tim who had to go around with the stick,
prodding the boat away from the side, giving it new
missions to undertake, new voyages to set out upon, while
Uncle James remained over on the other side, "back at
base HQ, following it on the charts," as he put it—which
meant a bench by the refreshment stall and long dips into
the *Daily News*. And it wasn't the trotting about that Tim
minded. He could have done that all day. It was the lack
of someone by his side to discuss those new missions and
voyages with, someone to work out the details with and, if
necessary, argue any point of disagreement by the old, old
method of wrestling it out on the grass.

On the other hand, there were times, Tim was sure,
when Uncle James felt the lack of some of *his* friends:
men like Mr. Irving Feldman, with whom he could play
pool on the brand-new table, or Mr. Martin Peel, who
could have provided him with a much sharper game of
gin rummy than any Tim could learn to play.

But of course it was out of the question inviting
anybody else along: boy, girl, man or woman. The secret
just had to be kept to themselves and there wasn't any
point in even discussing the matter. Tim knew this. Yet
such thoughts must have shown on his face from time
to time, or in the tone of his voice, just as they showed on
Uncle James's face or in *his* voice.

"Are you sure now there's nothing else you want?" the
man would ask at such moments. "Are you *quite* sure now,
my boy, because you've only to say the word."

Knowing that it wouldn't be as easy as that—that no

amount of money could put this little matter right—Tim would simply shake his head and try to smile and busy himself with what he was doing.

Then Uncle James, who was never fooled in such matters as this, would persist. Again and again he would repeat the question, until Tim began to feel fed up and even a little annoyed and, being of Irish stock, *show* he was a little annoyed. Upon which, Uncle James, who was also of Irish stock, would get annoyed himself—and show it.

"Well for the dear Lord's sake stop pressing them electric window buttons!" he'd snap, if they were out in the car. "Up and down, up and down, leaking the air-conditioning, knocking the divil out of the batteries!"

"Argh, the divil take the batteries then!" Tim would retort. "And anyway, I'd rather have the fresh air than your old air-conditioning!"

Luckily, at this point they would usually catch each other's eye and burst out laughing, and Uncle James would put his foot down and overtake the next three cars, making up hilarious stories about each of the drivers in turn until Tim was bucking helplessly in his seat belt, laughing so hard that there'd be tears running down his cheeks, and entirely forgetting for a while how good it would be to have some of the other kids along too.

Sometimes, however, the secret winners' sense of dissatisfaction would have nothing to do with lack of other companions. Sometimes it would simply have to do with being rich. Before the second week was out, for instance, they discovered that when a slight mechanical fault paralyzes a whole expensive model railroad system it becomes a major nuisance, and is not to be compared to a slight mechanical fault in some homemade or secondhand toy that can be cured with a kick or simply forgotten about. They also learned in that same week that a dent in the fender of a brand-new Cadillac, made by a careless driver in some parking lot, can be far more upsetting than a worse dent in the fender of some old jalopy.

Then again there was the food trouble. The rich new delicacies they tried never seemed to go wrong with Tim.

"Sure it must be the bowels of a blue-blooded aristocrat you've got inside ya, Tim, me boy!" Uncle James would marvel. But:

"Arrrgh, that fancy fish we had for breakfast's been with me all day," he would groan, "and it's giving me agonies! Slip into the bathroom and mix me some Alka Seltzer, there's a dear lad!"

Such were the things that went wrong at first. But although they were important as warnings and reminders that money wasn't everything, they were none of them as alarming as the times when their secret was in danger of being found out.

Like the afternoon they were caught in a traffic jam in their huge gleaming car—Uncle James resplendent in his straw hat, wig, and purple-green-and-white blazer, Tim wearing a black sweat shirt with a skull and crossbones on the front and the words *Hell's Angels* on the back—only six blocks from home. . . .

CHAPTER ELEVEN

Narrow Escapes

THEY HAD BEEN to Playland Park at Rye and they were coming back down Second Avenue on their way back to the new apartment. But instead of turning off and heading for Fifth Avenue while they were well to the north of their own home neighborhood, Uncle James had this crazy idea.

"Tell you what. Why don't we drive down further before we turn off?"

Tim stared at him. "But—but that'll take us near home, won't it?"

"I know, I know. But I've always wanted to see what the old place looks like from the seat of a Cadillac, and me hands and me foot is itching something terrible to steer her that way."

Tim felt a tingle of excitement run through his legs, just as it had done back at Playland on some of the big rides. It was the sort of tingle you get when horrified and delighted at the same time—with the delight steadily winning.

"Yes, but what if someone sees us?" he said, hoping Uncle James would have a good answer.

Uncle James had one, all right.

He laughed softly.

"We'll not be dawdling, you know. We'll not be parking it outside the supermarket and polishing up the hood

84

or something. We'll just be barreling through. And who'd recognize us from the bit of a fleeting glimpse they'll be getting? Especially in these duds."

Tim still wasn't *quite* sure.

"Yeah, well. . . . They may not recognize *you*. But *I* don't look all that different."

"So all right, boy—just you keep your head down if we see anyone we know. . . ."

Tim nodded. He felt happy now. And as they entered their own familiar territory he could hardly keep bobbing his head down for laughing, as they passed first one then another person they knew.

"If it ain't Mrs. Schultz!" Uncle James would announce, tipping his hat to a completely unsuspecting neighbor on the sidewalk, who didn't even give the car a second glance. "Why—and there's little Sharon O'Rourke. . . ."

So they drove on, not too slowly, roaring and bubbling with laughter, Uncle James tipping his hat and Tim ducking his head, until the man said, "Ah well, enough's enough! We'd better not push our luck too far, my boy. We'll turn off here."

And that's when it happened.

By the time they had turned into the side street leading west they saw too late the blockage ahead—caused by a huge green van that had stalled, slap across the street from sidewalk to sidewalk. Already there were two cars and a taxi held up in front of them.

"How the heck did he manage to get stuck in that position?" murmured Tim, feeling nothing more than mildly curious at that point.

"I don't know," grunted Uncle James, throwing an arm across the back of the seat and peering behind them. "But I do know we'd better be . . . Uh-huh!"

Now there were several cars behind them. Horns were

being hooted impatiently. All hope of any quick retreat back into Second Avenue was gone.

"We're stuck, my boy, good and stuck. Let's be hoping that truck driver can get her moving again fast!"

Neither of them was laughing now. Uncle James had his hand ready on the brim of his hat, true enough—but ready to pull it lower over his eyes, not to tip it in a gesture of gay mockery. As for Tim, he slumped further and further down in the seat, wishing he'd something to cover *his* eyes and face with.

"If only they'd stop blasting away on their horns!" moaned Uncle James. "It's fetching folks from all over the neighborhood."

Then suddenly he flung out a hand and gripped Tim's arm.

"Great God in heaven!" he gasped. "Get down, boy, down! Here comes your aunt!"

Tim dived like a duck after worms, pretending to search for something on the floor. With only his backside in full view it was a fairly safe bet that his aunt wouldn't recognize him—especially in a pair of pants she'd never seen on him before. But her own husband—was it possible she could pass within a few inches of *him,* trapped in the car, and not recognize him?

Out of the corner of his eye, the boy looked up at the man. Sweat was streaming down Uncle James's face as he tugged at the brim of his hat. His breathing grew heavier and quicker, giving Tim a good but far from comfortable idea of just how near his aunt was getting.

"Your face, Uncle," whispered Tim, suddenly inspired. "Be dabbing at the sweat on your face with your handkerchief!"

Feverishly, the man began groping about in his pockets.

"Here, quick!" said Tim, fumbling in his own pocket.

"Use mine!"

"Arragh, thanks, me boy!" whispered his uncle, grasping the piece of cloth. "And be saying yer prayers. She's practically upon us."

It seemed like an hour before the dabbing, sweating, grunting, groaning man finally slumped back in his seat and sighed with relief.

"Thank heavens for that, thank heavens for that!" was all he could mutter at first. Then he suddenly turned on Tim. "And what the divil d'you think it is *you're* laughing at? Hysterics is it, or what?"

Tim was almost choking as he pointed to his uncle's face.

"Yu-you're face!" he gasped. "Oh gee just look at your face! Nu-no wonder—heh! heh!—she didn't recognize you! It was the rag I used to wipe the mud off the fender with I gave you by mistake!"

Uncle James's face slowly cracked in a grin as he looked in the mirror.

"It's as stripy as my blazer!" he cried. "It's a zebra she must have thought was at the wheel—though I don't believe she gave us so much as a glance when it came to it. I—"

"You gonna stay parked here all day, feller?" growled a man with a cab driver's peaked cap, pushing his face through the side window. "C'm on, move it, will ya? Some of us have work to do."

The stalled van was already on its way around the corner.

"Sorry, my good man!" sang Uncle James, getting cheeky in his vast relief. "Why don't you retire young, like me?"

"Yergh! Ya rich slob!" the cabbie bawled after them, as they picked up speed and swept off. "Ya never did a day's work in ya life!"

On another occasion it was a traffic jam once again that was nearly their undoing. Certainly it was a long way from their home neighborhood (*that* was a mistake they never repeated), but in this case it was more a question of time than position, as they fumed and sweated in a snarl-up on the Tappan Zee Bridge. They had been out for a picnic on Bear Mountain and had left it rather late in any case—and now here they were, stuck for nearly an hour and not getting free until almost five thirty.

"What shall we say?"

"Leave it to me, my boy. I don't know yet, but whatever you do, leave all the talking to me. I'll think of something."

Fortunately for them, Aunt Bridget herself had been held up at work, helping with last-minute preparations for a party Mrs. Van Elst had only just that day decided to hold. When she made this clear—greeting them with "Here I come in, after working late, tired out, and you're nowhere to be seen, neither of you!"—Uncle James saw his opening.

"That's just it, my dear. You being late. We got worried and went out looking for you."

Tim blushed with shame.

It wasn't always the car that got them into difficulties. Once it was sheer forgetfulness on Uncle James's part—leaving on his expensive rope-soled sneakers after an afternoon's boating and not realizing this until he was back home and taking them off to put on the rack by the door. Luckily, Aunt Bridget was busy in the kitchen and didn't spot them—giving him the chance to scoop them up and smuggle them into his clothes closet for the night and replace them with a spare pair of work shoes.

On another occasion it was Tim's forgetfulness—coming to light when he pulled out his handkerchief as they were sitting down to supper and a roll of dollar bills fell out of his pocket onto the floor. True, it was only a small roll; but it was impossibly large for *him* to explain, as far as his aunt was concerned. To make matters worse, he didn't even know he'd dropped it. Only Uncle James—almost petrified—saw it, a mere few inches from his wife's feet, next to her chair.

As he told Tim afterward, "I just didn't know what to do for a minute, my boy! I couldn't get up and go pick it up, or she'd have spotted it at once, with the eyes of a hawk *she's* got. Yet there was no telling when she might not look down herself, to check if the rug was straight or something."

"So that's why you slid!"

"That, my boy, is why I slid, further and further down in my chair, trying to get my feet past your feet and hook the roll in and under and out of sight. And that, my boy, is how I came to slide a bit *too* far down on the chair, forgetting all the polish she puts on the durn things, until I went slithering under meself with that hell of a wallop and her thinking I'd been drinking or something. Ya laughing at?"

"I—I'm sorry, Uncle. It was just so funny! It—"

"Well it made sure her attention wasn't on that side of the floor anyway. And it gave me the chance of snatching the roll up as if it had come out of my own pocket, in the crash. . . . But listen to me, boy. Just remember—we can't be too careful about such matters. You mark that now!"

One of the strangest instances of near-disaster had nothing to do with carelessness in the ordinary sense. It happened when Aunt Bridget was passing behind Uncle James's chair one evening and she stopped and sniffed.

"What's *this* I smell?"

Uncle James didn't even look up from his paper, so secure was he feeling at that moment.

"What smell, my love?" he murmured absently.

"A sort of perfume. . . ." She sniffed sharply, then exclaimed. "Why! It's coming from you!" She bent over him. "Yes! Whatever is it?"

Poor Uncle James then rolled a wary eye up at her and did a little sniffing himself, but it was obvious that he still couldn't smell anything unusual and all at once Tim realized why. It was one of his uncle's ideas of luxury to lather himself with the costliest soaps whenever he took a shower over at the Fifth Avenue apartment. In fact he was actually beginning to *smell* like a rich man! Naturally, he and the boy had grown used to it; but, equally naturally, Aunt Bridget hadn't.

"Is it a soap smell, Aunt Bridget?" Tim asked, hoping his uncle would take the hint and could think of another of his instant explanations.

Uncle James did.

And he could.

"Ah, yes, my dear!" he said, with a slight start. "It'll be the apartment where we was working today. The soap in there. I washed my hands with it when we were through. I remember now."

It was quite truthful, of course, and it convinced his wife, who merely grunted and said something about not being able to beat "the good honest old-fashioned carbolic" in soaps. But they took the warning to heart, and from then on Uncle James contented himself with a plain odorless soap.

"I've said it before and I'll say it again, my boy," he whispered afterward. "We can't be too careful. We just *cannot* be too careful!"

But there are times when, no matter how careful you may be, things happen outside your control, things a person just can't be expected to take into account. The traffic jam on the Tappan Zee Bridge had been one of those things, and that had seemed bad enough. Yet it was nothing—absolutely nothing—to the blow fate handed out the day Uncle James took it into his head to tell some of his tales, to an audience of kids, in Central Park.

CHAPTER TWELVE

The Storyteller

IT HAD BEEN the usual pattern at the boating lake that morning. Uncle James had done two brisk circuits, striding around the edge and bellowing instructions to the imaginary crew; and then he had retired to "base naval HQ to study the charts and attend to grand strategy." In other words, he was sitting on a bench by the refreshment stand with his sailor cap tipped forward on his head, the *Daily News* in his hand, and a king-size carton of Coke at his elbow.

Tim, still trotting around giving his boat a prod whenever it touched the edge, was beginning to get a little fed up.

"I'll tell you what," he said, as he went past base naval HQ on his fifth circuit, "some of the crew are beginning to mutter. There's talk of mutiny."

As he'd expected, that helped to rekindle a little interest in his uncle's heart. But only a little.

"Is that so now?" was all the man said, glancing up from his newspaper. "Tell the dogs I'll have 'em swinging from the yardarms if there's anymore of it."

The next time around, Tim said with slightly more bitterness, "They're saying you're like all the rest—all big admirals everywhere. You're nothing but an armchair sailor, getting fat while they risk their lives in hurricanes and things."

Again Uncle James responded. But again not vigorously enough for his nephew.

"Take their names and stop their rum ration," was all he said this time. "And tell 'em there'll be a court-martial and mass floggings when they get back in port."

What's the use? Tim was thinking, halfway around on his next circuit. He's just too old to play for long. He's more interested in his old paper any day. . . . I wish Terry and some of the others were here!

And he was just making up his mind to suggest packing up and going somewhere else, when a real-live mutiny broke out close behind him.

He turned and stared. The wailing and screaming and bawling that had suddenly shattered the peace of the morning was coming from a crowd of small children, quite young ones, boys and girls, none of them over the age of about six and most much younger than that. They were all clustered around the big bronze statue of Hans Christian Andersen, sitting in his old frock coat and reading from a great bronze book. Tim had passed this place many times before on his trips to the park and had even lingered there, pretending not to listen, when someone from the public library had been reading stories for the little ones. Now, for the first time, he felt he could understand the look on the statue's face. It's as if he's gotten a headache with all this yelling, he thought, grinning.

But then his grin faded as he saw that the kids were really serious, really upset, and not just kicking up a din for the fun of it. Some were nearly purple in the face as they stamped and bawled; others were kicking at their nurses or mothers as these grown-ups tried to quiet them; one kid was banging his tiny fist on the open pages of the bronze book and screaming something in the statue's ear; and a little girl was bending down and having angry words with the bronze duck that stood at the statue's feet.

"What goes on?" a passerby asked one of the women who were struggling to calm the kids down.

"I don't know who started it," said the woman, hug-

ging her little girl close and stifling the sobs in the folds of
her dress. "But suddenly it flared up."

"Yes, but why?"

"Well—okay, honey, don't cry anymore—this is where
they sometimes send people from the public library to
read stories to the kids, and one of them—I think it was
the red-haired one up there, just trying to beat the statue's
brains out—he got it into his head that this was the day,
and the word seemed to go round in a flash, and they
gathered around, and they just wouldn't believe it when
we said there *was* no nice lady coming today, and they
waited, and suddenly—*this!* . . . No, honey, please, now
don't be silly. . . ."

The passerby shrugged and went on his way, looking
a bit bewildered and muttering something about "student
disorder even at *their* age!" But Tim was grinning again.
As the riot continued and the bawling and screaming got
louder, he felt like cheering. He didn't know what sort of
storytellers the New York Public Library usually sent
across, but he did know this:

*That just opposite the statue, on the other side of the
lake, feeling a bit at a loose end and bored with life, there
happened to be one of the finest storytellers in the whole
wide world—a storyteller who, miraculously, was all the
finer for never being allowed to practice his art freely at
home.*

He picked up his boat and went hurrying back to
naval HQ.

Uncle James looked up, one eyebrow raised at the boat.

"The crew have deserted, have they?" he said, chew-
ing on a yawn.

"Never mind the boat or the crew, Uncle," said Timothy. "There's real trouble over there. A real ruckus. Hear
that yelling?"

Uncle James blinked. A brighter glint came into his
eyes.

"Indeed I do," he said. "Don't tell me it's for real? Why—" he threw down his newspaper "—if it's someone over there harming the children we'd better be having a chat with him!"

"No, no, Uncle. Nothing like that. It's not a bodyguard they're wanting. It's a storyteller."

"A—a storyteller? You mean they want someone to tell 'em stories? They want it so bad they're in *that* state? Well now, Timothy my boy, you've applied to the right guy and that's for sure. You have indeed. Why don't we go over there right now and see what we can do to dry away them little tears. D'you think we should give 'em The Great Bull of Basham for starters, or is that a little too old? . . . No matter, we'll see, we'll see. . . . Maybe the Great Gold Crown of King Brian Boru would be better. . . ."

When Uncle James reached the scene—his sailor hat at a jaunty angle and the sideburns of his wig seeming to bristle with eagerness—the noise and confusion were greater than ever. The boy who'd climbed onto the statue to bawl in its ear was now straddling Hans Christian Andersen's shoulders and belaboring his head as if it were a drum. The little girl who'd been speaking sharply to the bronze duck was now beating it with a stick she'd found. Some of the kids who'd been kicking their nurses' shins were still at it—but getting slapped back in exchange. In fact there were now adult cries—of pain, of rage, of despair—added to the children's, and the din was terrific, so great that Uncle James had to cup his hands and bellow as if he were a real admiral trying to quell a mutiny with the aid of a loud-hailer.

"Whisht! Whisht! There! There! Your Uncle James is here to—ouch!"

A little boy had taken a kick at him, while another was tugging at the knee of his white pants, as if to drag him out of the way. Tim began to wonder if he'd done the right thing after all.

"Now listen, *will* yez? Little children, dear little children—stop that now, d'ye hear, young feller, or I'll t'row ya to the sharks! Listen, *please!* Your Uncle James is here to tell you all the stories—ALL THE STORIES—y' ever want to hear. If you'll just settle down—YEAH, STORIES, STORIES—I'll be making a start on the first of them. . . ."

As the man had suspected, the one word *stories* was worth five thousand others at that moment. The first time he'd uttered it, there had been a distinct dropping-off in the activity around him, with one little boy stopping his kicking and raising a tear-stained face in hope, and the other relaxing his grip on the knee of that now rather crumpled pair of pants. At the second utterance of the word, bawled with all the force of Uncle James's lungs, another dozen paused in their yelling and turned to look. And at the third—double—bellowing of the magic word even the kid on the statue began to climb down, with an eager look on his face.

There was still quite a bit of crying, but it was nothing like as loud as it had been a minute or so before. Nurses and mothers, sensing victory, quietly drew their children toward them as they sat down on benches around the statue. Small thumbs strayed toward small mouths. Small wet eyes that had been shut tight with fury now came fluttering open and, opening, went wide as they focused on the tall man who looked like a sailor and talked like a cop, calmly hitching his pants and sitting on the statue's knee.

"That's better . . . that's much much better now . . . that's a real lot of fine young men and women y'are where a minute ago there was nothing but a bunch of babies. . . . No, little girl, leave the duck alone now; he wants to hear my stories just as much as you do. . . .

There. Now listen. Seeing as how ye're all behaving like
proper little ladies and gentlemen I'll tell you a story I
wouldn't be telling to babies for fear they'd get too scared.
You see, it's about this bull, this great big fearsome bull
that lived long, long ago and once upon a time in the
beautiful country of Ireland . . ."

So he began to tell them of the Great Bull of Basham,
and after the first few words whatever sobbing and whin-
ing had still been going on quieted down to a moaning.
And after the next few words this moaning fell to a
sniveling. And after the next few words there was perfect
quiet, save for the sucking of thumbs and the traffic noises
from across the park.

Nurses and mothers began to relax, to breathe more
easily. Children began nestling even closer to them.
Others began—very, very quietly—to creep nearer to the
feet of the statue, the bronze duck, and the gently swinging leg of Uncle James, as he sat there spinning his tale.
And all at once, what had been an ugly noisy riot became
a scene of delight, of peace, of enchantment, with the sunlight falling in soft patterns through the leaves of the
nearby trees, onto the heads and the cheeks of the children, helping to dry the tears they'd forgotten about,
and bringing an extra sparkle to their eyes and their open
lips.

Uncle James told many tales that morning. As he said
to Tim later, "With an audience like that, how can a man
ever stop till he runs short of breath and his throat dries
up?"

Some of the stories, like the one about the Great Bull
of Basham, were genuine Irish folktales. Some, like the
one about the Great Gold Crown of King Brian Boru,
sounded Irish and were about genuine Irish heroes, but
were really what Uncle James had made up and added to
over the years.

And some—as the kids grew more and more enthusi-

astic and he grew happier and happier—were what he'd
made up on the spot. Like The Dragon that Lived Under
Manhattan (and caused steam to rise from the manhole
covers as he prowled hungrily below, trying to find a way
into Central Park and the plump little boys and girls he
knew were there). Or like the one about the Long Island
little men (who caused trains to run late, and switched off
the fans and air-conditioning on hot days). Or like the
favorite of them all—*which he had to tell three times
over*—about the war of the statues (waged at night between Hans Christian Andersen and his duck and the
Alice in Wonderland group of statues across the lake).

Nothing like it could ever have been heard in Central
Park before: the lilting, swinging, loudening-and-soften-
ing voice of Uncle James; the gasps and the giggles and
the great bursting cheers of the kids; the cries for more;
the even greater bursts of cheering when the man said,
"Okay, okay. Just one more time. And Tim, would ye be
fetching me another large Coke to pour on the coals in me
throat, there's a lovely boy?"

For that was another thing. The more the kids responded the more did Uncle James. A gasp in the right
place would set him lowering his voice even deeper and
rolling his eyes even wilder and conjuring up even greater
dangers for his heroes. A laugh would be greeted with a
twist in the tale that was even funnier than before, and
when this got the kids laughing all the louder he'd throw
in another twist that would have them screaming and
sobbing and almost crying again with mirth. As for the
cheering and the shouting for more—he just couldn't
resist it.

So, as tale followed tale, and the crowd grew larger
and larger until the path at the side of the lake was
blocked and the cop who came to clear it fell under the
spell himself and just sat there stock-still on his horse,

drinking in every word—Tim realized he'd never felt happier in the whole of the time since they'd won the money. And when they finally managed to break away from the protesting—but *cheerfully* protesting—children, it didn't strike him as being at all strange that Uncle James should voice that very thought.

"Tim, me boy," he croaked, as they made their way to the refreshment stall, "believe it or not, but this is the happiest morning I've spent since we heard the great news. It's—well—you know what they say about it being better to give than receive?"

Tim nodded. A slight cloud crossed his own happiness at that point, as he remembered Aunt Bridget and the presents he'd tried to give her at the time of the "eccentric millionaire."

"Well," continued Uncle James, "so it *is* better to give than receive. . . . But, dammit—" he gave a wheezy cackle and did a little shuffling jig that nearly took him over the edge, into the lake "—it's even better to give out of your heart than your pocket, if you see what I mean."

Tim smiled. "I sure do, Uncle!" he said. "You were great back there. You gave those kids the time of their lives."

"Argh, it was nothin'!" said Uncle James, with a flourishing tug at his cap and a swagger that was the absolute opposite of the modesty of his words. "It did me good to be able to get the tales off me chest so nice and free without worrying a single once about whether your aunt was listening or not."

Again Tim smiled. But again the cloud crossed his happiness.

He thought at the time that it was just the mention of his aunt once more. But later that day he was to wonder if it hadn't been a sudden glimpse into the future he'd been given, just like one of the heroes his uncle had been

talking about. No magic stone had chuckled out a sinister
message. No strange bird had flown down onto his shoulder and whispered in his ear. But, looking back, it seemed
to Tim that even as his uncle was speaking those last
words, there had come with the cloud a warning: a
warning that they'd not heard the last about that storytelling session.

CHAPTER THIRTEEN

The Storyteller Rides Again

AUNT BRIDGET was not in the best of moods that evening. She looked more tired and drawn than usual when she came in, and was quick to find fault with things that were trivial, even for her. So their shoes were in the rack? All right. But why hadn't her husband's been placed neatly side by side, instead of one at either end? And what was Tim's left shoe doing with its lace trailing half across the floor? And even though Uncle James had been careful to place the sheet over the flower-patterned chair, couldn't he have done it a little tidier, without getting creases all over it?

"Argh, she'll be asking us to put newspapers over the sheet next!" sighed the man, when she had gone into the kitchen to start fixing the meal.

"And that's enough of *your* lip, James O'Connell!" came his wife's voice. "I'm not stone-deaf, you know, even if I am dog-tired."

Uncle James rolled his eyes and winked at Tim.

"I think it's time for the news," he said meekly, switching on the television.

"So long as it *is* the news," came Aunt Bridget's voice, "and none of that cowboy nonsense or that Mars rubbish or that navy stuff or any of those other fairy tales they try to pass off as adult entertainment!"

"Of course it's the news, my dear," murmured Uncle James. "We wouldn't dream of watching or listening to fairy tales, would we, Tim?"

But, that one little joke apart, there wasn't much to
cheer them on the news either—unless they could have
squeezed some fun out of the flooding of a subway, or a
strike of welfare workers, or a long dull statement from a
mayoral candidate, or an interview with a sanitation offi-
cial, or the story of a body that had been fished out of the
East River. Even so, they continued to wink and grin at
each other, still feeling the effects of their morning
triumph.

"If this is good wholesome television news," said Uncle
James at one point, not bothering overmuch to keep his
voice down, "give me 'My Favorite Martian' any day of
the week."

"Now that's enough of that!" came the snapback from
the kitchen. "You know very well what I mean!"

To which Uncle James, in his high spirits, replied with
a silent display of derisive laughter—a battery of winks
and slaps on the knee and doublings-up—as if to say, "See
how she rose to *that* one!"

In fact it was while he was going through this panto-
mime, with Tim not knowing whether to laugh at him or
look the other way, scared stiff that his aunt might come
back into the room and catch his uncle at it, that the news
suddenly took a brighter turn—a brighter turn for the
general viewer, that is—but a most alarming one for Tim
and Uncle James.

". . . We hear a great deal these days about student
unrest," the reporter was saying, "and about its spreading
even into the high schools . . ."

Neither the boy nor the man was bothering to glance
at the screen—so familiar did the topic sound. Instead,
Uncle James was going through the motions of being sick
with laughing, and Tim was still keeping an anxious eye
on the door.

". . . but over in Central Park today . . ."

Even that brought only a flicker of a glance from Tim and nothing at all from his doubled-up uncle.

". . . passersby witnessed what must surely be the youngest student rebellion ever to be staged."

At this point, Tim did turn his head sharply—just in time to see the picture change from the close-up face of the reporter and split up into patterns of light and shade to show a crowd scene.

"It happened at the Hans Christian Andersen Memorial. Apparently, word had gotten around among the children that there was to be a storytelling session there, and when no one showed up, the kids got angry. . . ."

"Uncle—," whispered Tim, managing at last to tear his horrified gaze away from the screen.

But the warning was unnecessary. Uncle James was frozen in midlaugh, his head forward, his eyes bulging, going almost walleyed in his attempt to watch both the screen and the kitchen door at the same time.

"Unfortunately," came the reporter's voice, "we hadn't a camera crew on the spot when the riot started . . ."

A great big sigh came gushing from Uncle James's lips.

". . . but we were lucky enough to get a few clips from some student moviemakers who were in the vicinity testing some newly designed hand equipment."

Something like a moan grew out of the sigh.

"They too weren't in time for the riot, but they did manage to take these pictures of the man who saved the day, a gentleman who happened to be passing, saw what was needed, and stepped in to fill the bill most handsomely. . . ."

Now the picture changed. Instead of a distant crowd scene—a picture of any crowd in any parklike setting—the camera zoomed in to show the children gathered around the statue and, mercilessly, it continued to close in until there was a perfect picture of Uncle James on the screen, sailor hat a-tilt, blazer buttons gleaming, leg casually swinging.

"May God grant—," began Uncle James, in a hoarse whisper.

He was going to say, "May God grant they didn't have proper sound equipment with them!"—but it was too late.

"And so, every night, when the stars twinkled in the sky and on the lake," came the lilting unmistakable voice of Uncle James, straight out of the screen, *"the Statues would go into battle. And at first things didn't go so well for the old gentleman whose knee you see me sitting upon, because he was so bulky, and he made so big a splash every time he moved in the water, and his coattails would float up and shine in the moonlight . . ."*

"Will you be quiet in there, James!" came Aunt Bridget's voice from the kitchen. "I can't hear the news for you!"

Uncle James gave a little shudder and looked ready to faint. For Tim, however, the voice of his aunt broke the spell. He knew her well and he realized that it would be only a matter of seconds before she'd be in to add a frown and a sharply wagging finger to her words. He also realized that so long as she didn't see the screen they were safe, that she was convinced that the recorded voice of Uncle James was his real voice, uttered live.

Quickly the boy darted across to the set and, with his finger on the on-off switch, he waved frantically at his uncle.

"I'm telling you now," came his aunt's voice again. "Stop that blethering! I can't hear the news for you!"

Even as she spoke, Tim was whispering, "Keep on with the story, Uncle. When I switch off. Keep on with the same story."

A faint gleam of hope came into the man's eyes. Tim took a risk, trusting that his message had got across. He switched it off. There was a slight pause. Then, with

something like a groan in his voice, Uncle James picked up
where his image on the screen had broken off.

". . . And so—and so it was the little old duck here—
the little old duck that saved him and helped to win the
war. Because the little old duck was like all ordinary
ducks everywhere—you see—he could swim under water.
And it was he who acted as a submarine, and when the
Mad Hatter and his buddies came swimming across it
was the duck that came up at 'em from under, nipping
their knees and their toes with his hard bronze beak—
and—and—"

"What—" Aunt Bridget was back in the room now,
wiping her hands on a towel and glaring down at Uncle
James "—what is all this tommyrot you're filling the lad's
head with *this* time? How many times do I have to tell
you, James O'Connell, that tales of that kind will do
nothing but soften his brain and make him useless for life
as a man? How many—?" She suddenly noticed the
blank television screen. "And turning off the news to do it,
too! Turning off the only sensible, wholesome sort of
program they ever put out on that thing, just to fill his
head with a pack of lying nonsense about statues that
come to life in the dark! Timothy, switch it on again.
Right now."

"M-ma'am?"

"The television, boy, the television. Switch it back on
again."

"It—it—"

"Oh, come out of the way!"

Aunt Bridget brushed him aside and switched it on
herself. Then, as the set warmed up, Uncle James sank
deeper and deeper into his chair and Tim stood staring at
the screen, his fingers tightly crossed and his toes all
curled back, wishing and wishing he had the power of
some of his science-fiction heroes to destroy a television
picture with the intensity of his stare.

So they remained, the woman fuming, the man silently praying, and the boy staring until his eyes burned, as the spot grew larger and larger and unfolded into a picture, and the voice found its way out of the crackling.

But they needn't have worried. Uncle James had left the screen. The scene had changed from Central Park to City Hall, where a group of people were marching up and down waving slogans on picket boards. And the voice was that of a councilman complaining about the water supply in his part of town.

"Statues walking in lakes at night!" said Aunt Bridget, in tones of disgust. "When there's all this trouble in the world that the lad has to find out about!"

"Yes, dear," said Uncle James meekly, sadly, and even gratefully.

"So let's have no more of it."

"No, dear."

"As for you, Timothy, don't look so miserable. You'll thank me for it later."

Tim nodded and kept his eyes down.

But it wasn't his aunt's attitude toward storytelling that made him feel so dejected just then. It wasn't even the dreary subject the councilman was talking about on the television. It was the sudden thickening and blackening of the morning's cloud—the knowledge that they could never really be happy with their money until they could think of a way of getting Aunt Bridget to share it.

Her face, as she stared down at the set, nodding severely at the councilman's points, was paler than ever. Under her eyes, the skin was a yellowish blue, and puffy. Tim thought he had never seen her look so tired, so far from ever smiling again. And all at once he swore to himself that whatever else they did—he and his uncle—they must find a way of making her life easier.

CHAPTER FOURTEEN

"We'll confess..."

"I KNOW, my boy, I know! Don't think I haven't been worrying about it myself. It's been weighing on my mind heavier every day."

It was the morning following Uncle James's television appearance and they were sitting in their Fifth Avenue apartment discussing the problem of Aunt Bridget. Outside it was gloomy—gray and steamy after a rainstorm—and all the wide view did just then was to magnify the gloom. Inside it wasn't much better. Neither of them had bothered to turn on any of the lights, either in the many reading lamps scattered about the apartment or in the concealed strips cunningly built into the walls and sills and corners at great expense and in a variety of soft shades, ranging from Early Morning Lemon to Late Night Peach.

They hadn't even bothered to change into any of their new clothes, if it came to that. Uncle James had on his old faded dime-store check shirt and Tim his everyday jeans and sneakers, and neither felt at all inclined to touch the breakfast they had ordered. On the table at the side, Tim's favorite mint ice cream with chocolate chips slowly melted in its silver bowl, while Uncle James's striped bass grew cold and greasy.

And the same spirit seemed to have settled over everything else in the apartment. Uncle James's wig, which the

previous afternoon had been placed jauntily over a beautiful ebony glove showing all the stars and planets ("Just
the size of my head, my boy!")—the wig had somehow
shrunk and shrunk during the night until it had slid off
into a sad, crumpled little heap of gray-white fur at the
foot of the globe, causing Uncle James to groan and say,
"Hurtled all the way down from the heavens above, and
that's how it is with me heart!"

Elsewhere it was as if the same gloomy spell had been
cast on the other objects. The train set lay still and silent,
the locomotive on its side and the coaches scattered here
and there behind it. The lid from the box of disguises had
been left half off, revealing a set of Vampire Fangs and a
false nose that suddenly seemed funny no longer—and not
even frightening. Just sad. A crumpled Ping-Pong ball lay
on the rug near Tim's feet, and a pack of trick playing
cards were scattered on the small table next to Uncle
James's chair—but the ball might have been an old ciga-
rette pack and the cards a handful of used railroad tickets
for all the memories of fun and games they stirred just
then.

"I suppose we'd better be thinking of tidying the place
up," said Tim, with a sigh.

"Whisht! Whisht!" Uncle James put out a hand and
pushed him gently back into his chair. "One thing at a
time, my boy. . . . It's the major problem I'm thinking
about at the moment and it's no use running away from it
any longer, now is it?"

Tim nodded and waited, but without much hope. His
uncle still had the slumped despairing look of a man
who'd run out of ideas.

"It's—it's—" Uncle James shook his head, as if he'd
started running out of words as well. Then, clenching his
fist and waving it at the ceiling, he suddenly braced
himself and declared, "But I'll tell you what! I'll tell you

now just where it's at, lad. If something doesn't happen
soon—if we don't come up with a way of getting her to
share the money, and to feel the benefit of it, knowing or
unknowing where it came from—then by everything
that's holy—" he brought his fist crashing down on the
trick playing cards, scattering them even further "—we'll
have to make a clean breast of it!"

Tim stared. "You mean tell her?"

"I mean tell her!"

"Everything?"

"Every little thing. And the divil take the money! If
she makes us give it all over to one of her ould charities,
so be it."

Tim nodded. The gloom was as thick as before, but
somehow it didn't seem quite so heavy.

"But of course," said Uncle James, speaking softer
now, "it would be much better if we could think of
something that made such action unnecessary."

"Yes," murmured Tim.

"So let us think," said Uncle James, placing his right
elbow on his right knee and putting his forehead into his
cupped hand—much as if he'd said, "Let us pray."

For about five more gloomy minutes they sat there
thinking hard. Or trying to think hard. The furthest Tim
himself could get was to see his aunt's face again, looking
all drawn and tired, as he'd seen it the night before. As for
Uncle James, he appeared to have done no better.

"Argh, be damned, my boy!" he said, giving his head a
rough shake and sitting back. "It's no use forcing it. Ideas
like that—ideas of the sort *we're* after—they come like
angels in the night. Softly. Without warning. Unan-
nounced . . ."

"But—but there may not be an idea at all. There may
be no answer at all, Uncle."

"I know. I know. We'll just have to hope there is and

be patient. Tell you what—" he slapped his knee "—we'll give ourselves till next week—till—till next Tuesday evening. If it doesn't come by then we'll know it never will. And then we'll confess. We'll tell her everything. Over the supper table."

Nothing they did that next week was at all enjoyable. The weather picked up, the sun shone again on leaves and grass and water, on the shiny peak of the sailor cap, on the gleaming hood of their car, on the whole of Manhattan stretched out before them, but the gloom remained in their hearts. Nothing they ate or drank or smelled gave them any pleasure. Not once did they experience any of the earlier thrill it had given them to step out of their old neighborhood and into the life of luxury. And there wasn't even the same excitement—the same tingle they'd had before, when they felt themselves on the brink of being found out.

For instance, several people in the old neighborhood— even in the same apartment building—had seen the television news broadcast, and they had all remarked on the resemblance between the storyteller and Uncle James. But that's as far as it had gone. To those people it was just another part of the general-viewer's game of "Don't he look like so-and-so?" Nobody suspected for one second that the debonair gentleman with the sailor hat and silver sideburns really was Uncle James.

"But what does it matter now, boy, whether they did or not?" said the man, the following Tuesday afternoon. "Seeing that inside a couple of hours she'll be hearing all about it from our very own lips!"

Being found out, however, is very much easier than owning up—as the two discovered that evening. Since they'd started their new life they had often come to the table back home with small appetites—usually because of the amount of delicacies they'd been consuming during the day, or as a result of some narrow escape they'd just had, putting them off their food for a while. But tonight it was worse than ever. It was as much as either could do to look at the food and take a fork to it, so nervous had they begun to feel.

"Well," said Aunt Bridget, putting her own fork down and staring at them. "I don't know what's the matter with you two these days, I really don't. . . ."

"Oh?" said Uncle James weakly, making a brave attempt to suck in a strand or two of spaghetti.

"I—I feel fine, Aunt," said Tim, lifting up a few strands himself.

"You're not eating the half of what you usually do, and going about with not a word for anyone, and so pale. . . . Both of you, I mean . . ."

"Ar?" grunted Uncle James, gulping down the spaghetti and feeling himself go three shades paler still.

"Yes," said Aunt Bridget. She was still staring at them, but with the hard lines of her face softened a little, in an expression of genuine concern.

Tim felt like flinging down his fork and confessing there and then. Indeed, he might have, had not his aunt continued.

"Mrs. Van Elst was saying only today she thought *I* wasn't looking so good lately and wondering if I oughtn't to be taking things easier. . . . But *you* two—"

"Argh! Oh! Hey! Did she now?"

Tim turned in surprise at the sudden change in his uncle's manner. Why, there was something like the old sparkle in those blue eyes again!

"She said that, my dear, did she? Would she have been thinking of giving you lighter duties now?"

Aunt Bridget sniffed. "Light duties, light duties! That's

all you can think of, James O'Connell. . . . No. Not she.
She's a fine woman but she likes value for her money and
who's to blame her? . . . No, she was probably thinking
of cutting down my hours and getting someone else. . . ."
Aunt Bridget's cheek twitched and she hung her head a
little. She too now seemed to have no appetite left, judging from the way she pushed back her plate. "And—and if
she was to do that I just don't know where we'd all be.
Heaven knows, it's hard enough as it is. . . ."

Uncle James was positively smiling now. Tim felt
shocked.

"But maybe you've misjudged the dear good lady, my
love. Maybe she really is thinking of putting you on
lighter work. Important work, responsible work, mind,"
added Uncle James, cocking his head craftily as he
watched his wife's bowed head. "But lighter."

"I never," said Aunt Bridget softly but firmly, "mis-
judge anyone."

"But this time, what with feeling out of sorts and all,
maybe you have. In fact I feel *sure* you have, me darling,
and your ould James isn't a bad judge of character either.
Why, I—"

"James O'Connell, will you stop talking rubbish?" His
wife was glaring at him with some of her usual ferocity.
Then she bent her head again and her voice softened once
more, as she went on, "I know you're concerned about me,
and I know you wish it was so—that Mrs. Van Elst *was*
planning something of the sort. But it *is* only wishing.
. . . I know the lady. You don't. She'd never dream of
doing such a thing. And there's an end to it."

There was a silence for a few moments. Then Uncle
James shrugged.

"Ah, well!" he murmured. "You never know."

And he proceeded to shovel in the spaghetti with
something remarkably like his old gusto.

Tim watched him with amazement—an amazement that didn't leave him until ten minutes later, after his aunt had gone into the kitchen with the dirty plates and the noise of the running water arose, and Uncle James had leaned forward, gripped his arm, and whispered:

"I have it, my boy, I have it! The dear angel I was telling y' about visited me through the very mouth of your aunt. . . . The idea, lad, the great idea! . . . It came wafting like blossom on the wind of her words!"

CHAPTER FIFTEEN

The Great Idea

UNCLE JAMES outlined his idea the next morning, over breakfast in the Fifth Avenue apartment. He was in top form again. He had showered with a brand-new soap called Killarney Clover, changed into his brightest blazer, donned his wig, brushed up his sideburns, ordered fresh finnon haddock, Irish bacon and German sausages, kicked the busted Ping-Pong ball under the sofa, out of sight, and turned the piped music up to nearly full volume, having put in a special request for a couple of cassettes devoted to reels and jigs.

"So what *is* this great idea you've had, Uncle?" pleaded Tim, still feeling doubtful himself. "Come on—or I'll go straight out and into the park without you."

"Patience, patience, patience, lad!" said his uncle, waving a forkful of the soft succulent fish in time with his words, which themselves were in time with the lilting background music. "I've just been adding a few finishing touches to it in me head—a dab of butter here, a sprinkle of fine salt there—"

"I'm talking about this idea, Uncle—not your breakfast."

"So'm I, my boy, so'm I," munched Uncle James. "You sure you won't try a morsel of this fish? It's—"

"Look!" cried Tim, standing up. "It's about fifteen hours now since the idea came to you—so you said—and I think it's time you were telling me *roughly* what it's all about, don't you?"

"Okay, okay. Sit down, sit down. I guess it's all ticking away perfect now, anyways. . . . Listen. . . ."

Tim sat down. He waved away the silver dish his uncle was pushing forward.

"The idea," he said.

"The idea," said Uncle James, nodding gravely. "Well, it all hinges on Mrs. Van Elst. Something your aunt was saying last night about that lady being such a hard-nosed old—er—lady. She—"

"I didn't hear Aunt Bridget say that."

"Not in them exact words, my boy, no. But that's what she meant all right when she said the old—er—lady liked to get value for money out of her staff. The plain fact of the matter is of course that she's been making a patsy out of your aunt for years. All these last-minute calls for extra duties—these parties she suddenly takes it into her head to give. What happens? She bends her finger and your aunt goes off at a trot to do the extra work—tired as she may be. I tell you, Mrs. Van Elst is nothing but a hard-nosed ould—"

"But she pays my aunt for this extra work, doesn't she?"

"Yeah! Sure! But only at the basic rate. Which ain't very high, not for a worker of your aunt's quality. A rate which ain't once been raised these past ten years."

"Aunt Bridget doesn't seem to mind."

"No, because your aunt's a fool, my boy—though, here, don't go quoting me on this, now will you? . . . Anyways, that's the setup. But—," Uncle James broke off to lift the lid from the bacon and sausages, sniff deeply, and chuckle. "But these things cut two ways, my boy, and that's what's at the basis of the idea the angels sent me last night. You see, if your Aunt Bridget did break down from overwork Mrs. Van Elst would suffer too. Your aunt's the last of her kind, you see. Maids and cleaners just don't come like that anymore. Yet—" Uncle James munched on a mouthful of sausage and bacon and waved time to the music, indicating he didn't want to be interrupted "—yet—" he swallowed "—yet Mrs. Van Elst's too mean to let your aunt have lighter duties, with full pay, even for a few weeks till her health picks up. . . . Even though it would be for her own good in the long run. There *are* people like that, you know—the old country was full of 'em and they say England's just the—"

"Yes. Okay. I understand. So?"

"So listen. . . . If someone propositioned Mrs. Van Elst and said—" Uncle James drew himself up and put on his best Fifth Avenue voice " '—See here, my good lady, you put Mrs. O'Connell on lighter duties and *we'll* pay you the money to pay her with'—why!" Uncle James became himself again. "Why, the hard-nosed old biddy, she'd jump at the chance! Something for nothing! Wouldn't be able to resist it!"

Tim nodded. Slowly, he was beginning to see the reason for his uncle's cheerfulness. Even so . . .

"Wouldn't she wonder what it was all about, though?"

"Not if we said it's in the terms of someone's will—an old uncle of hers who knows Bridget would never take any straight handouts. . . . You leave that side of things to the lawyer feller we've got. He'll handle it. You'll see. . . ."

And see Tim did. Uncle James spent the rest of the morning down at the lawyer's office, and when he came back he was rubbing his hands.

"A beautiful young feller, that!" he said. "A young feller right after me own heart!"

"He's doing it then?" asked Tim.

"Doing it? He's done it, my boy. Smooth as clock-work."

"Mrs. Van Elst agrees?"

"With bells on! I tell you—it was an angel sent me

that idea, an angel who must have known all the parties concerned. I mean for one thing the lawyer feller turned out to be an old friend of the Van Elst family. He was courting the daughter of the ould harridan till she turned him down—the mother, I'm talking about—for not having good enough prospects. So he was only too glad to put the proposition and she was only too glad to listen, feeling maybe she'd been wrong about him now that he's a big-time lawyer and all. . . ."

"So it's all set? From today?"

"From this very morning, my boy. This very minute your aunt's doing something nice and gentle like taking the dog for a walk or counting the silver, instead of sweating her soul out over the scrubbing and polishing and whatnot. . . . Mind you, she drove a hard bargain, old mother Van Elst did. You know what she says? She says to the lawyer, 'Well yes, that's all very well, but I still have to find someone to do the heavy work Bridget was doing. . . .' So in the end he had to agree to pay Bridget's full wages *and* the full wages of the person who's to replace her."

"It's worth it, though, isn't it?"

"Of *course* it's worth it! You'll see, tonight, when she gets home from work looking all rested instead of worn out. . . . Meanwhile, why don't we go and celebrate over in the zoo. We'll have lunch there and toss a few nuts to the monkeys. Not the ordinary peanuts, mind. Some of these fancy macadamia nuts at two ninety the bottle. We'll bring a little joy into the lives of *them* poor caged creatures, too!"

So they fed the monkeys and sailed their boat and went for a drive in the car and stopped off at the Palisades Amusement Park and ate ice cream and cotton candy and all in all it was just like old times again—like those golden earlier days of their new life. And by the time they'd changed back into their everyday clothes and were waiting for Aunt Bridget to come home it was a very much brighter pair than the two who'd waited for her the previous evening.

"Now whatever you do, don't let it slip out that we know the least little thing about today's change, will you?"

"No, Uncle. But don't forget to act normal yourself. You keep breaking out into smiles. Cool it."

"I know, I know. It's with the pleasure of contemplating the beauty of my idea. But I'll be as straight-faced as that old statue in the park, you see if I won't! I'll—*whisht!* I do believe the dear lady herself is about to join us. . . ."

He was right. And if he'd had any secret fears about being able to keep that straight face, they must have melted the moment she entered.

Indeed, if anything, she looked sadder and sicker than on the previous night.

Uncle James was so shocked he nearly gave everything away.

"Surely to heaven, my dear, you can't *still* be feeling tired?"

"Tired? Tired?" Aunt Bridget paused in her routine glance around the room. "What makes you think I'm tired?"

"Well—I—well—I mean—well I'm going by the look on your face, my love."

Aunt Bridget sniffed.

"Well I'm not what you might call as fresh as a daisy. But tired, no. Just . . ." She sat down by the table and started drumming with her fingers on the surface. "Just troubled," she said, staring into the wall behind her husband's back. "Very troubled."

"Oh . . . *troubled,* did you say?"

She nodded, tight-lipped, still staring into the wall as if it were a screen on which there was being shown some approaching tragedy.

Uncle James cast a puzzled look at Tim and gave a slight shrug.

"And—and why should you be troubled, my dear?" he asked gently.

"I'd always considered Mrs. Van Elst to be an honest woman," said Aunt Bridget, still staring at the wall. "A bit on the hard side, it's true, but honest and upstanding. Now I ain't so sure. . . ."

"Oh? . . . Oh? . . . Oh?" They came out like a series of little coughs. "And why is it you're not sure, then?"

"If she doesn't like my cleaning," said Aunt Bridget, raising her voice and giving him an angry glance, as if it were all his fault, "why doesn't she tell me so straight out? Eh? *Why?*"

"But what makes you think that, my love? Has she been hinting she doesn't like your cleaning, God forgive her for a fool?"

"No, it's—I'll thank you to watch your language, James! I've trouble enough without that. . . . It's just that she's taken me off my usual work and put me on to 'light duties'. . . ."

Aunt Bridget said the last two words with great scorn, then resumed her staring into the imaginary screen. Uncle James rolled an eye at Tim and brightened up.

"Well then, isn't that the Good Lord himself heard what we was saying last night and went and whispered the words into Mrs. Van Elst's ear, the darling lady? You should be rejoicing, my dear, it's just what the doctor ordered. . . . Isn't it?"

"No. It is not. Least, it's what I *could* do to be having for a spell—these light duties. But as *I* was saying last

night, it's just not like Mrs. Van Elst. Not on the same rate
of pay, the way she's insisting. I tell you there's something
wrong, something—well I don't think she's telling the
truth, and that's the fact."

"Maybe—maybe the good woman's seen the error of
her ways, my dear. Maybe she's trying to make up for
overworking you in the past."

"Hrrmph!" was all Aunt Bridget replied to that, still
staring at the wall, still looking worried, still drumming
lightly on the tabletop.

As Uncle James knew from years of experience, argu-
ing with his wife on such a subject wasn't the least bit of
use. So he held his peace and told Tim to do the same.

"It must have come as a shock to her system after all
these years," he said. "Give her a day or two and she'll
start picking up. Like a flower that's been transplanted
into richer soil, she's wilting a bit. But give her a day or
two, my boy, and we'll be seeing a beautiful difference."

But, as each day's end came around, the wilting of
Aunt Bridget grew worse and worse until, on the following Monday evening, she simply dropped her packages at
the door and came stumbling in, sobbing. *Still*—Tim
noticed, with a curling shiver down the back of his neck—
with her shoes on!

"My dear, my dear!" cried Uncle James, helping her
down onto the chair. "Whatever in the world has happened? You look as if you've just seen a terrible accident.
. . . There, there! . . . Whisht, now, whisht!"

He nodded to Tim to get the water boiled and a cup of
tea made, then went on holding her around the shoulders
while she sobbed.

"Tell us," he murmured, "tell us what it is, my dear.
Tell your old Jim. . . ."

This made the sobs come crashing through her fingers

all the louder. Tim stared in horror. Never had he seen his
aunt cry before, and from the look on Uncle James's face
it was a long time since he had, either.

"Just tell us, my love, just cough it up and you'll feel so
much the better."

"I—I—*I've quit!*" cried Aunt Bridget at last. "I—I—
I—*I've quit my job with Mrs. Van Elst!*"

For a few moments her sobs came faster than ever,
while Uncle James and Tim stared at each other in be-
wilderment. Then she began to calm down.

"It—it's just that I can't be a party to dishonesty," she
said, sniffing and wiping her eyes and shaking her husband's arm from her shoulders. "And Mrs. Van Elst—she
was being dishonest. . . ."

"Dishonest, my dear?"

"Yes. I challenged her straight-out this morning. I
said, 'Mrs. Van Elst, why are you doing this, giving me
lighter duties for the same pay? It ain't like you and I say
that with all respect but I must know or I quit!' . . . I—
I decided on them words last night, while you were
asleep. . . . And then—you know what she says? She
gives me some old story about an old uncle leaving me
some money and getting it to me through her. You never
heard such rubbish!" She was dry-eyed now and flushed—
much more like her old self. "So I decided there was some
very bad case of dishonesty here, worse than I'd thought,
and if you want my opinion it's all to do with taxes, it's a
way of dodging the taxes, so I quit."

Uncle James let out a deep long breath and did a little
wall-staring himself.

"Well," he said. "Well. . . . Well. . . . Of all the—"

What he was going to say, Tim never got to know. All
he did know was that it sounded like something angry,
something not altogether in Aunt Bridget's favor. But just
then she started sobbing again, and her husband softened.

"Take it easy now, take it easy. Maybe it's all for the
good—"

"But—but what shall we do without the money? How shall we manage on just yours?"

Uncle James flashed a quick wink at Tim, over her shaking shoulder.

"We'll find a way, my dear. Don't worry. And at least it'll be giving you a rest. . . . Tim, I think the water's boiling. And Tim, just see what there is in the icebox. . . . We'll make the supper tonight while your aunt takes things easy for a change."

"D'you think she'll be all right?" asked Tim, when his aunt had gone to wash up.

"Sure!" said Uncle James. "Sure! It's just shook her up, that's all. And what I said about a rest's true."

"Yes, but you heard her. You know how she worries. She'll never rest till she's made up the money she used to get from Mrs. Van Elst."

"I know that. But part of it I can make up by saying I've had a raise at work. Not all of it, of course, or she'll get suspicious. But enough to calm her down a bit and keep her from scurrying around looking for any old job. As I say, at least she'll be getting a bit of a rest."

"But what then? When she starts worrying again? Which'll probably be in a day or two at the most."

Uncle James shrugged, but he was smiling again as he tapped Tim on the chest with the butter knife.

"Listen," he said. "If the dear angels could send us that last idea—which nearly worked, you mark *that*—well then, they can just as easily be sending us another."

Tim wasn't so sure. He nodded and tried not to show his anxiety, but he just wasn't as sure as Uncle James. It seemed very much to the boy as though those "angels" the man was always talking about were every bit as ready to hand out parcels of trouble as good ideas. Even readier, if it came to a straight count. . . .

And, before the next forty-eight hours had passed, he had cause to remember this.

CHAPTER SIXTEEN

A New Problem

"I JUST THOUGHT I'd better mention it, sir."

"You did quite right, Jenkins, quite right."

"The management are very keen on that sort of thing, where it's bachelors and other single gentlemen."

"I'm sure they must be, and who's to blame them?"

"They just like to know that things are being looked after with reasonable care."

"I'd be the same myself."

"And without a woman around—"

"Say no more, Mr. Jenkins. We'll look into it right away."

This exchange took place the next morning in the lobby of the Fifth Avenue apartment building, with Mr. Jenkins looking rather embarrassed.

"Well isn't that the very divil!" groaned Uncle James, as soon as they were in the elevator. "Here's the management dropping their hints that we'd better be getting a cleaning lady to keep the place tidy, and there's your aunt out of her main job and worrying herself stiff."

"But we can't ask *her*, Uncle," said Tim.

"I know we can't, boy. But it's the irony. Because whoever does get the job of cleaning for us is on to a cushy number. After all, we don't sleep here and most days we're never in for more than an hour or so. I tell ya . . . the gods can be downright wicked cruel at times."

After they'd changed, Tim said, "It doesn't look so bad to me. Do we *have* to have someone to clean?"

Uncle James glanced around.

"Well I don't know about not looking so bad. There's your old socks on the floor over there for a start, and model railroad coaches all over the place, and that rug's been kicked up like that for over a week, and you could write your last will and testament in the dust on top of the grand pianner. . . ." He sighed. "I guess it would never do for your aunt."

"Yes, but—"

"Or for the management, the way Jenkins was talking. No, we'd better be hiring a woman for half a day a week or so, before we get thrown out. After all—huh!—we can afford it."

He went over to the telephone and dialed the lobby.

"Ah, Mr. Jenkins. . . . I been thinking about what you said. . . . Is there any of the ladies already cleaning on the premises you think would like to take on our little pad a half day a week? . . . What's that? . . . Well couldn't you ask around? We'll pay top rates you can tell them. Maybe more. . . . Yeah, so long as they do a good job." Uncle James winked at Tim as he continued, "We come from a home where the standards in such matters is very high!"

He shook his head sadly as he put down the phone.

"It's as I've always said, my boy. It's not everyone wants a cleaning job these days. I keep trying to tell your aunt that. 'Take it easy,' I keep telling her. 'Nobody's gonna fire you for taking it easier than you do. Women like you's too hard to get.'"

"Doesn't Mr. Jenkins know of anyone then?"

"Not off hand. Most the cleaners here is all booked up—and very choosey, from what I gather. But he's gonna ask around."

"Well that's okay then. We're trying, aren't we?"

"Eh? . . . Oh, yes, sure! . . . Only it's just that I

can't get over the irony of it, my boy, the sheer hard lines of it. Because just think, when we do find someone— just think how cushy she'll be having it with employers like *us*. Rich, handsome, generous to a fault, who require only a little light dusting and tidying and will be inclined to leave her champagne and lobster for midmorning snacks instead of coffee and cookies. And there's your aunt, cleaning for some slave-driving old trout like Mrs. Van Elst, and probably getting just such another when she finds a substitute. I tell ya: Sometimes life is cruel." He sighed and snapped off a red carnation from a vaseful of them. "Anyways," he said, sticking the flower in his blazer buttonhole and admiring the effect through the dust on the mirror, "let's forget about our servant problems for the time being. How does a little drive up to West Point grab you?"

When they returned, late that afternoon, Jenkins was there to remind them again.

"I'm afraid we drew a blank, sir, here."

"Oh?"

"About the cleaning lady. Mrs. Rivera who does three of the apartments here said she might think about it when 15C leave in October, but that's as close as I could get."

"Argh, well, you tried, man, you tried," said Uncle James, slipping him a crumpled five-dollar bill.

"Thank you, sir!" Mr. Jenkins brightened up in a flash. "It's a pity about Mrs. Rivera, she's probably the best cleaning woman in the whole of Manhattan—"

"Pardon me!" Uncle James coughed politely into his hand. "The second best, maybe. Not, I think, the best. Oh dear, no! Eh, Tim?"

"Er—if you're thinking of who I'm thinking of, Uncle—no."

Mr. Jenkins looked somewhat bewildered. "You know of someone then?"

Uncle James shook his head and sighed.

"Ah, no, not really, Mr. Jenkins. Merely a wistful dream. . . . You were saying about Mrs. Rivera?"

"Well, she is good, but she's just not available. However . . ." Mr. Jenkins looked down at the bill, still crumpled, in his hand, and began to smooth it out ". . . she did say she'd ask her sister, who's nearly as good as her, who cleans somewhere uptown, and who might decide to make the journey down, if she likes the sound of it, and if Mrs. Rivera can remember to tell her when she goes home tonight."

"Here," said Uncle James, pulling out another five-dollar bill. "Tell her to make a note of it on that."

As they changed into their everyday clothes up in the apartment, Uncle James glanced around and said, "Well, I'll warrant the old place'll look a sight tidier tomorrow afternoon at this time."

"You think Mrs. Rivera's sister will come then?"

"It won't be for want of remembering to ask her, if she doesn't. And when she sees the way we have with five-dollar bills it won't surprise me if Mrs. Rivera herself doesn't change her mind."

But, as often happened, Uncle James turned out to have been overoptimistic. Mr. Jenkins shook his head when asked the following morning if he'd any news for them.

"Not really, sir, I'm afraid. But Mrs. Rivera says her sister was interested to hear of the job, and she's considering it."

"Maybe," said Tim, as he watched his uncle putting on his wig upstairs, "maybe you should have given Mrs. Rivera a *ten*-dollar bill to make a note on."

"Maybe," murmured Uncle James. He licked his fingers and fluffed up the sideburns. "Maybe that's what I will have to do in the end, if we don't hear soon. I must say, though, now my attention's been drawn to it, the dust

of the place is beginning to get on me nerves. If only—
huh! Now who can this be?"

He went over to the telephone.

"Ah, Mr. Jenkins. . . . You *have?*" Up went Uncle
James's thumb and down went his right eyebrow in a
joyous wink that sent Tim running to the other phone to
share the good news. "Well now," he heard his uncle say,
"that's great! Just great! This'll be Mrs. Rivera's sister, I
take it?"

"Well, no, sir," came Mr. Jenkins's voice. "Not exactly.
You see, she thought it over and thought it over but
decided it was too far just for the half-day after all. . . .
However, she did know of a really first-class cleaner just
thrown out of a job—not her fault—a most deserving
case—" For some reason, Tim felt his heart begin to
thump. "And she managed to get word to her, only in this
last hour, sir, and the lady's come straight over." Jenkins
lowered his voice. "I must say she looks very respectable.
She's waiting in the lobby now. Shall I send her up?"

"Of course, of course!" came Uncle James's voice,
crackling in Tim's left ear and booming jovially in the
right. "Send the dear woman right up and we'll see what
she's made of. I feel in an interviewing mood this
morning."

"Very good, sir."

After the receivers had been replaced, Tim came out
of his trance.

"Uncle!" he gasped.

"Yes, my boy?"

"What if—what if—?"

"Spit it out, my boy. What if what?"

"What if this lady turns out to be—*to be Aunt
Bridget?*"

"Hoh! hoh! hoh!" guffawed Uncle James, throwing his
head back so hard it caused his wig to slip. "Whatever
makes you think—awp!"

He suddenly gulped and looked far from happy.

"Maybe we'd better—here—hold on. Whatever you do, don't answer the door. . . ."

Feverishly, he dialed the doorman.

"Jenkins, is that you? . . . Good! Now listen. . . . Is she still there? . . . The elevator door's just closed, has it? . . . Well, listen, did she tell you her name? . . . She did? And it was—oh *no!* . . . It *can't* be! Hang on. . . ."

Uncle James clapped a hand over the mouthpiece and turned to the boy.

"You're right!" he croaked. " 'Tis herself! And the elevator's on its way already!"

CHAPTER SEVENTEEN

The Emergency

"Look, Jenkins, man. . . . For the love of God did ye tell her my name? . . . You didn't? You're sure? You just said 12D? . . . God bless ye for that! . . . Well now, listen. I've a feeling we're not going to be in, never mind why, I just don't feel like interviewing after all. And when she leaves—ahhhhhh!"

The exclamation escaped from Uncle James's throat like the last air from a toy balloon. It was caused by the ringing of the chimes at the door. He replaced the telephone gingerly, with one finger to his lips, but not without making a rattling sound, so shaky was the hand that held the instrument.

"Leave it!" he whispered, seeing Tim moving hesitantly toward the door. "Don't go near it! We're not in."

"But—"

"Whisht!"

Sweat was running down the man's face as he motioned Tim to keep still.

"Oh merciful heavens!" he breathed, closing his eyes and almost sinking to his knees as the bell went again. "Oh, please, God, send her away and about her business!"

"Hello!" came the unmistakable voice from the other side of the door. "Is anyone home in there?"

Uncle James kept his eyes shut tight. And as the chimes rang yet again he lifted his hands to his ears, obviously intending to shut the sound out also.

133

But those hands never reached those ears. The right one came pretty close but the left one encountered an obstacle on the way: the corner of the Monster Box of Everyboy's Master Disguises, which had been left untidily overhanging the edge of the sideboard.

With horror, with fascination, with shivering horror and freezing fascination, Tim watched, unable to do anything, as Uncle James, still with his eyes shut, made a groping clutch at the toppling box: a frantic movement that sent the box blundering into the vase of carnations, which went over with a vivid red splash and a crash.

At any other time it might have been amusing—and certainly interesting—to see the pattern made on the sideboard and rug by the crimson flowers and the fragments of glass and the false noses and beards and teeth and sticks of greasepaint.

But not now. . . .

"Hello! Hello! Are you all right in there?" came Aunt Bridget's voice, with an insistent ring in it they knew of old.

There'd be no shaking her off now, thought Tim, staring at his uncle in agony, hoping and praying that the man's quick wits wouldn't fail them this time, but fearing in his heart that here was one crisis that would prove too much even for *them.*

And then it came. . . .

As Tim stared ·at the tight-shut eyes, the vacantly gaping mouth, the disarranged wig, and the debris of flowers and false features, an idea began to unfold, rapidly but distinctly.

He tiptoed across, even as it was still forming.

"Listen," he whispered, shaking his uncle's arm, "this could just work. And what have we to lose? . . . Use one of your other voices and tell her to wait a minute."

"Are you crazy?" whispered his uncle.

"Are you all right in there?" called Aunt Bridget. *"Sir!"* she added.

This gave Tim extra encouragement.

"Tell her!" he whispered. "Tell her you'll be ready in a minute! . . . If you don't, I'll open the door right now!" he growled, making as if to move off.

"Wait! No! . . . What was it you wanted me to say?"

"That you'll be out in a minute. In your lawyer-type voice. . . . Then come into the bedroom with me and I'll tell you how we can get around this beautifully."

"Hello in there! Are you all right?"

"Go on!" Tim gave his uncle a thump in the arm.

With a little groan, the man opened his eyes.

"Just—just a minute! I'll be out in a minute!"

It wasn't his *best* lawyer voice, but Tim decided it would do for the time being.

"Thank you, sir. I was just wondering . . ." came the voice of Aunt Bridget in reply. "I'm sorry if I woke you up."

"There," said Tim, dragging his uncle into the bedroom. "You've passed the first test. She doesn't recognize the voice."

"No—but—"

"Listen. Here are your sunglasses. Put 'em on. Tell her you're half-blind. That's how you came to knock the vase over. Okay?"

"Yes, but won't she?—"

"Be quiet while I tell you, Uncle, *please!* Now get your wig straight . . . and here—just hold everything a second. . . ."

Tim darted back into the other room, bent over the scattered disguises and selected a bushy moustache and a bottle of gum.

"Here—stick this on."

"But it's nearly black!"

"I know. But men's hair does go gray before their

moustaches anyway. **Come on.** . . . Not *that* way up. Here—let me."

Quickly he arranged the moustache, gave its ends a twirl, then stepped back.

"Why, I wouldn't know you myself!" he gasped.

Uncle James lifted his sunglasses an inch and took a closer look in the mirror. His mouth twitched under the black hair.

"I'll be damned if *I* would either, my boy!" he said, grinning. "Well now, this is beginning to make sense!"

"Great! I was hoping you'd think that. Because you still have a lot to do on your own, Uncle. Here—put this dressing gown on. It looks like it's coming in handy after all. . . . But wait. Just give me time to pull down the venetian blinds and get behind the drapes and you can go and let her in. . . . It'll be nice and dim in there and remember—you have eye trouble. That's why you like the blinds down and wear dark glasses."

"God bless you, me boy, for the mother and father of all great and famous good ideas!" murmured Uncle James, following Tim and cautiously drawing the drapes an extra foot or two to make sure the boy would be well concealed. "If the angel hasn't come to you himself with this one!"

"The voice!" hissed Tim, pushing him forward. "Just let her in and remember the voice. Hey—and listen—before you go . . ."

It was indeed as if an angel were whispering to him just then, such a glow did he feel all at once.

"What, my boy?"

"Why don't we hire her?"

"Eh?"

"Don't just get rid of her. *Hire* her. She needn't ever see you here again, after this. It would solve the big problem, wouldn't it?"

The mouth under the moustache fell open in awe. Then the eyes behind the dark glasses lit up with joy.

"Tim," whispered Uncle James, "Tim, me boy, if this comes off—"

"Are you all right still, sir?"

Uncle James gulped.

"Wish me luck!" he murmured.

Then he crossed the darkened room, padding cautiously to the door.

CHAPTER EIGHTEEN

Interview in the Shadows

THE ONE GREAT advantage of making up such a plan on the spur of the moment is that you never have time to worry about the sheer outrageous boldness of it, or about the possible snags. Had Tim had time to think about it more he might never have risked hiding behind the drapes, for instance. He might have decided instead to play for complete safety and lock himself in one of the bathrooms—so putting at least two closed doors between himself and the scene in the living room.

But it was a scene he didn't want to miss—partly from pure natural interest, and partly to be close at hand in case of emergencies. What *he* could do to save the situation if his aunt should see through Uncle James's disguise, or if his uncle should say or do something to arouse her suspicions, Tim didn't know. And even if he *could* think of something in such a case, how on earth would he be able to intervene without giving himself away, too?

The question flitted through his head even as he settled himself in the corner behind the drapes and plucked at the edge to make himself a chink to see through, but he didn't bother to try to find an answer. Instead, he contented himself with the knowledge that— thanks to having pulled down the blinds just behind him—it was a dark enough corner, with the added advantage of having the piano between him and the rest of the room to give extra camouflage. All he hoped was that his aunt and uncle would sit someplace where he could see them both in the angle formed by the raised lid of the instrument. There'd be no chance to move his position once his aunt was in the room, for that would mean moving the drapes slightly—a risk he just daren't take.

Above all, though, his thoughts were centered on the glorious achievement it would be if the plan did come off. To be able to give Aunt Bridget a job—a nice soft well-paid job—*that* would come so near to solving their great problem as to be worth taking almost any risk. *If only . . . if only . . .* With these two words racing through his mind, he crossed his fingers hard and held his breath as Uncle James opened the door.

If only—he meant—*Uncle James doesn't blow it. . . . If only we haven't overlooked something. . . . If only the idea's as good as it seemed when it first arrived. . . . If only we have a little bit of luck on our side. . . . If only the idea* had been *sent by an angel, and he's still got an interest in it. . . .*

"Come in, madam, come in!"

So far, so good. The voice was getting more lawyerlike with each word. And Uncle James had enough presence of mind not to hover by the door and let her see him close up too long.

"Please shut the door after you, madam," he was saying, as he hurried over to the deepest armchair in the room—the one with wings at the sides, Tim noted with relief. "I daren't stay in a draft too long."

"Oh dear, are you all right, sir?"

"Perfectly, perfectly. So long as I don't get in a draft. And—er—get too much strong sunlight. It's a rare eye disease I have, nothing catching, nothing serious, you understand, but a nuisance. Occulomyelitis. . . . Pray sit down and tell me about yourself. . . . The chair there, right behind you."

"Thank you, sir."

As Aunt Bridget sat down, Tim was glad to find she

came full in his field of vision. In the dimness it was rather difficult to see her expression in every detail, but he could tell from the way she kept her head slightly bowed that she was completely taken in by the lawyer voice.

"No, it's nothing serious," the man was going on, gaining confidence with every breath, it seemed to the boy. "A minor eye defect that runs in the family. Usually clears up by about noon, but until then—no strong light, no drafts. . . . You were saying about yourself?"

"Well, I've always given satisfaction with my cleaning, sir, and I can give you all the references in the world to say so, sir. And I am used to dealing with persons of standing, sir, like yourself—"

"Heeh! heeh! But I'm *sitting*, dear lady!"

Tim at this point rolled his eyes heavenward and hoped his uncle wasn't getting *too* confident.

"Excuse me, sir?"

"Hah! Nothing, nothing. Just a little joke. Person of standing. Sitting. Heh! Please continue."

"What I meant, sir," said Aunt Bridget, with a slight edge to her voice that made Tim wince, "was that I'm used to handling with great care valuable items of furniture and the like. . . ."

As she said this, she began to peer around, trying to judge the value of this apartment's contents. Again Tim was thankful for the dimness. He couldn't be sure, but for all he could remember there might be some of their everyday things scattered around. From now on—if this really worked—they'd have to be very careful about such matters as *that!*

"Well—ah, yes, naturally we—I—I should expect you to go easy on the priceless china and whatnot. But really, madam, we—that is, I—I'm not the fussy sort. I'm aware that accidents do happen. We shouldn't have you shot or anything like that!"

"Not with me, sir!"

Tim saw Uncle James stiffen at hearing such a well-known tone enter her voice.

"Eh? I beg your pardon?"

"Accidents. They don't happen where I clean, sir. In all my life I've never lost a single valuable cup or glass, not so much as an eggcup."

"Oh? Ah! Yes. To be sure. Good. Splendid. Well then, here's what I suggest. . . ."

Aunt Bridget sat up, very alert now, as the man began to outline his requirements.

"Shall we say—er—three half-days a week—never before noon, you understand?—of—ah—let me see—er . . ." Uncle James's voice tailed off. Tim noticed he'd sunk further into his chair and for a moment the boy had the terrifying thought that his uncle might have been finding the strain too much and was about to faint. "Is—is there something wrong, madam?" came his uncle's voice at last, sounding very feeble, from the shadows.

Then Tim saw that his aunt was staring hard—straight at the man—and he too felt suddenly feeble.

"No . . . no . . ." Aunt Bridget sounded a little puzzled. "I'm sorry, sir. Please forgive me for staring so. . . . But there was something in the way you were holding your head that reminded me of someone."

Down, further into the chair, slumped the man.

"Oh . . . er—who, may I ask?"

"Well to be honest with you, sir, and not to tell you any untruth, and certainly not meaning to be forward with you at all, but since you ask I have to tell you. It's my husband you reminded me of. . . . But only a little."

"Oh . . . ah . . . hmm . . . I see. . . ."

"No offense intended, sir."

"I should think not! . . . Ah! . . . That is, no offense received, madam."

"I mean he isn't at all as—well, as—as—"

"Handsome?"

"Well, *you* said it, sir. . . . *Dignified* was more the word. And of course he hasn't the head of hair on him you have, sir."

"Hmph!"

"And of course he would never in a million years get to be living in a place like this, more's the pity!"

"Oh, indeed?"

Now it was into the man's voice that an edge was creeping. Tim crossed his fingers harder than ever.

"No, sir. You see, he has it *in* him. He has it in him to do anything, be anything. But he's feckless, sir, if you know what I mean."

"No—I do not!"

"Well, to speak straight-out, sir, he's bone idle, lazy."

"Oh, *come* now, madam!"

"Well, maybe not *exactly* idle. But he don't have the drive that his brains deserve, if you see what I mean."

"Possibly, madam," said Uncle James, in his frostiest tones yet, "possibly the poor man has never had the encouragement that's so necessary for success."

Aunt Bridget dipped her head, probably realizing the argument had gone too far.

"I wouldn't know, sir."

"No, Mrs. O'Connell, so it would seem!"

Now the woman looked up again. Sharply.

Tim held his breath.

"How—how did you know my name, sir?"

"Huh? I—er—you said so, didn't you?"

She shook her head firmly. "No, sir. I did not."

"Well then—I—it must—I—"

Tim could have groaned aloud. Here, already, was an emergency. And already he could think of a perfectly good answer—*the* answer. But how to get it across to his gasping and floundering uncle? Then:

"Ah! Of course! The doorman. Mr. Jenkins. Dear Mr. Jenkins. He told me your name when he announced you. Over the phone."

Aunt Bridget nodded. "Oh, yes, sure, he must have. Yes. I see."

"Good old Jenkins. He never forgets to announce a visitor properly, no, not he. A splendid doorman. King of all doormen." Uncle James's voice had taken on a bubbling, buoyant quality in the vastness of his relief. "And once having heard your name," he continued, lilting ever upward, "how should I forget it, dear lady, seeing as it's my own as well?"

Tim's head began to reel. What on earth did his uncle think he was doing? Couldn't the man *ever* let well enough alone?

He hardly dared look at his aunt, as she said:

"Oh, really?"

"Why, sure. . . . And do you know what? I'll wager that that's where the resemblance comes from. The tilt of the head you noticed. I'll wager that I and that fine feller of yours are related—very distantly, you understand, because the O'Connell tribe must be very thick on the ground by now."

"His full name is James Oscar Errol O'Connell, sir," said Aunt Bridget, full of interest now. "Does any of them mean anything to you?"

"Hmm! Fine name, fine name—but no, I can't say it does. Irish-born, is he?"

"Belfast, sir. Came over as a young man. Me too."

The man shook his head.

"Hmm, no! My own branch now, they came over long before that. Time of the famine. Well-established old American family by now."

"Of course, sir. I wasn't presuming to claim any close relationship. . . ."

Tim could have danced for joy. Now that it had come off, he couldn't help recognizing Uncle James's startling confession as the masterstroke it was. From now on, whenever Aunt Bridget caught some resemblance to her husband, she'd put it down to this "distant relationship" and think no more about it.

But if it hadn't come off! . . . Tim put extra pressure on his sweatily crossed fingers and tried not to think about that.

"Anyway," said the man, in full confident spate, "this is all the more reason for hiring you. Anyone connected with the O'Connells—even by marriage," he couldn't resist adding, in a somewhat stern, somewhat haughty voice, "anyone of that name is bound to be good."

"I—I'll try my best, sir."

"I'm sure you will, Mrs. O'Connell. Now about terms and things—er—what is it *now?*"

Aunt Bridget was peering at something on the floor near her feet.

"Excuse me, sir, but isn't that a toy railroad train I see down there?"

"Oh—eh—ah—why, yes! We have them in these places for the mice and roaches, ha! ha!"

"Sir?"

"Just my little joke, Mrs. O'Connell. Think nothing of it. . . . But the train now, yes. Yes, that is a toy train. As a matter of fact it belongs to a nephew of mine—"

Again Tim broke into a sweat.

"The lad comes visiting and I like him to have something to play with."

"And very thoughtful of you, too, sir. . . . My, but I have a nephew who'd just love to play with that."

"Ah, yes, I'm sure, but hold it!" said Uncle James sharply. "There's to be no bringing him around here with you, you know."

"Oh dear, no, sir! I'd never dream of it! I was just saying—"

"It's not that *I* should mind, but my own nephew's a very nervous lad, a bit of a softy"—behind the drapes, Tim's mouth went hard and his eyes flashed—"a proper little milksop, in fact, scared of his own shadow, has fits when any strange boys come near him, especially rough boys!"

"Oh, but my Timothy isn't a rough boy!" Tim gave his aunt a silent kiss for that. "He's not a softy, either. He's very nice indeed."

"He's what, madam? Speak up, please. My ears are affected too, along with my eyes."

"He's a very nice boy indeed!"

"Who is?"

"Timothy, my own nephew."

"Good! good! No doubt he's glad to hear you say so—er—from time to time. . . . Anyway, don't let us write it off altogether. Maybe we'll be able to get them together one day. But only when I give permission, mind."

"Yes, sir. . . . What did you say your nephew was called?"

Tim closed his eyes and prayed. Would his uncle overdo it, this time? Two O'Connells were fine.

But two Tims could ruin everything. . . .

CHAPTER NINETEEN

Victory in Sight

"I DIDN'T SAY, as far as I can remember. But since you've asked, the name of my nephew is—er—" suddenly a leer came into Uncle James's voice "—Cuthbert!"

Tim was torn in two—overjoyed that his uncle hadn't made a mess of things, enraged at hearing himself called by a name like that.

"What a nice name for a young gentleman," said Aunt Bridget, not sounding any too thrilled herself. "But you were saying about the hours you'd like me to come, sir."

Uncle James cleared his throat and sat quiet for a few moments. They were now approaching the really tricky part of the interview and Tim was glad to note how respectfully his uncle seemed to be considering it. After all, the main object was to drive a very soft bargain indeed—to give Aunt Bridget the maximum amount of money for the minimum amount of work. Knowing her, the secret winners were well aware that this wasn't going to be easy. Then, to complicate matters, there was the additional fact that they had to settle on hours that were not going to make it too hard for them to come and go without bumping into her. . . .

Uncle James must have decided to tackle this side of the matter first.

"Well now, as you'll appreciate, Mrs. O'Connell, I wouldn't want you to be coming too early in the day, on account of my affliction."

"No, sir, of course not. You did say noon."

"Yes, well . . . that's really putting it at the outside.
. . ." (Uncle James was obviously thinking about the
latter end of the afternoon now. It wouldn't do to have
Aunt Bridget working in the apartment too late, when
they were wanting to come back and change into their
everyday clothes.) "I'll tell you what," he went on, "let's
say ten thirty. I'm usually feeling okay by then. And if
I'm not I'll just leave word with Jenkins that I'm not to be
disturbed. I'll pay you for any such waiting time, of
course," he added, hastily.

"That's very kind of you, sir," said Aunt Bridget. "And
ten thirty would suit me fine. It would give me time to
tidy up my own place properly, after the menfolk have
left for work and school. They're a very untidy pair."

"Oh, come now, Mrs. O'Connell. I'll warrant they're
tidier than most men, if you were to look into it. . . . But
anyway, that's settled then? A ten thirty start. . . . Now
if you were to go on until three thirty, that would make
five hours, would it not? . . . I'm afraid I can't let you
run to any longer than that because I usually have business to attend to here during the late afternoon. Very
important not to be disturbed."

"Oh, that would be fine, sir."

"And you don't mind working across the lunch hour?"

"Well, no, I could—"

"We—er—I'd see you were left some tasty sandwiches,
of course. And a flask of something stimulating. Are you a
drinking woman, Mrs. O'Connell?"

"Indeed not! I've never touched anything stronger
than Hawaiian Punch in my whole life!"

"Ah, well—you don't mind if I have drink about the
apartment, do you?"

"Oh no, sir! That's your business."

"Eh? Excuse me? My ears. . . . You were saying?"

*"What you take to drink, sir, is your business. Entirely.
I never like to impose my views—"*

"What? What? What's that?"

"*I never like to impose my views on my employers, sir.*"

"Oh! . . . Huh! . . . Hmm! . . . Well now, we've got it to a five-hour day. How about three days a week: Mondays, Wednesdays, Fridays?"

Aunt Bridget peered around.

"Well, sir, are you sure that wouldn't be too much? I am a very quick worker as well as thorough and I'm sure I could get through in one day. Two at the outside."

"Nonsense, nonsense!"

"Sir!" Aunt Bridget sat bolt upright. "I know my own job!"

"And I still say nonsense. I know what I like. Sure, most cleaning ladies might have it done in a day—*and* make a thorough job of it. Thorough by ordinary standards. But—but it's against my religious beliefs, if you must know."

"Sir?"

"Yes. It's against my religion to have people breaking their necks to be thorough as well as quick. My soul would roast in the eternal flames if just one of my employees ever got sick through working too fast. . . . And you look none too robust yourself, Mrs. O'Connell."

"But . . . what religion is this?"

"The Holy Tabernacle Convention of the Nine-Day Saints of St. Louis," said Uncle James, without pausing for breath or, Tim imagined, so much as blinking an eye. "And I trust you're a woman with respect for religious views, Mrs. O'Connell, even those belonging to other people?"

"Oh yes, sir—"

"Very well, that's settled then. Three days a week, Mondays, Wednesdays and Fridays, five hours each day. Okay?"

"Yes, sir."

"Starting at ten thirty unless otherwise requested. Agreed?"

"Yes, sir."

"At a rate of—let me see—ten dollars an hour?"

"*What?*"

Aunt Bridget shot straight up from her chair as if she'd been threatened. Then she sat down again and gave a faint giggle.

"Goodness me, sir! For a moment I thought you said ten dollars an hour!"

"So I did, Mrs. O'Connell, so I did."

"Oh, but that's out of the question, sir! No cleaning woman ever gets *that!*"

"Those chosen to clean for the Brothers of the Holy Tabernacle Convention of the Nine-Day Saints of St. Louis do!" said Uncle James grimly.

"Well I'm sorry then," said Aunt Bridget, getting up to go again. "I can't take the job. It would be like taking advantage of somebody else's religion and that's against *my* religion. A dollar seventy-five and fares is my rate."

"Tush, woman! Twaddle! Sit down, sit down. Don't you realize that you'll be working across your lunch hour and that rates double time in anyone's religion?"

"Yes, but—"

"Just sit down or you'll be having my eyes hurting me again."

She sat down. Tim's own eyes were hurting as they strained in the dimness to read his aunt's expression. Was she softening?

"So ten dollars it is, then?"

She shuddered, shaking her head.

"I'm sorry, sir. I couldn't dream of it. Taking the lunch-hour work into account, and also the fact that there's talk of a general raise, I might accept two fifteen."

"Two fifteen? Pah! I'd be expelled from the Brother-hood for even considering it. . . . But listen, there's more

to it than that. I'm a very fussy man, I may want to call on
you on one of the other days at a minute's notice, to come
and do some extra dusting, or some ironing, or—or bake
me an apple pie, or lay the table for a dinner party—or
something of the sort."

"Yes, sir, I'm used to that. The lady I did most of my
cleaning for up to last week was always asking me to
come in extra and I'd try to fit it in."

"Try? *Try?* . . . I want to be *sure*, Mrs. O'Connell. I
want to be sure that on the days you're not due here I'll be
able to get you at once."

"But I have one or two other small cleaning jobs, sir. I
may be busy on one of those—"

"That, my dear lady, is what I'm getting at. You must
resign from those jobs. If you work for me you must hold
yourself in readiness. Sure, sure! I know!" Uncle James
lifted a majestic hand. "You'll lose the money you might
have earned at these other places. . . . But that's where
my high rate comes in. It's to make up for loss of earnings
elsewhere. Doen't that make sense?"

"Well . . ."

Aunt Bridget still sounded doubtful—but she was obviously weakening.

"No . . ." she said. "Not ten dollars an hour."

"All right!" Uncle James knew when to bend a little.
"Seven then. Seven an hour. Mind you, you wouldn't have
to let me down. You really would have to stay home, or
near home, so that I know where you are, where I could
send for you at a minute's notice."

"Oh, I wouldn't let you down, sir!"

"That's fine, then. And listen—let's forget about call-
ing it so much an hour. It gives an entirely wrong impression. Why don't we call it a flat weekly wage of a hundred
dollars—for three days' work and four days' being in
readiness? Doesn't sound so very grand, put like that, does
it?" Uncle James rubbed his chin. "Maybe I ought to up it

to two hundred, or two hundred and fifty, perhaps."

"Oh dear, no, sir, no! That would really be too much!"

"All right. One hundred a week it is then. It makes me feel I'm taking a terrible advantage of you, Mrs. O'Connell, but if you insist—"

"I do! Indeed I do insist!"

"Okay. . . . Well, look—today's Wednesday, I know, but it's getting rather late. Why don't we leave everything until Monday and start the first week then, nice and straight?"

"That would be fine, sir, if you're sure you'll be all right till then."

"Sure I'm sure! What tidying up there is to do this week I'll get Cuthbert to do. It's time the young loafer did some work for a change."

Again the jubilant note was surging into Uncle James's voice. And no wonder! This time Tim didn't feel the least bit sore about the Cuthbert crack. Not after such a victory as this. And to add to his joy was the fact that for once Uncle James didn't appear to be getting too cocky in his triumph.

"I won't get up to let you out, if you don't mind, Mrs. O'Connell," the man said, sensibly staying where he was in the shadows of the deep armchair. "The draft from the door, you know . . ."

"That's quite all right, sir," said Aunt Bridget, standing up.

As she did so, her face became less dim, and Tim was thrilled to see how pleased and relieved she was looking.

"But if it wouldn't be too much trouble before you go," continued Uncle James, still with that dangerous lilt in his voice—quite drunk now with success, Tim could tell—"I wonder if you'd mind drawing the drapes across a little further and giving me a little more shade?"

"Certainly not, sir, a pleasure!" said Aunt Bridget, stalking straight toward the spot where Tim was.

Silently raging at his uncle's foolhardiness, Tim shrank further into the corner. As the footsteps came nearer he prayed hard that Aunt Bridget wouldn't take it into her head to look *behind* the drapes.

But she didn't and—as the cord was pulled—Tim couldn't help letting out a long thin sigh of relief. Fortunately, it blended with the swishing noise of the drapes.

Nevertheless, it wasn't until he'd heard the apartment door close behind his aunt and then the soft clash of the elevator doors outside that he dared to stick his head around the drapes—just in time to see Uncle James spring up, fling off the dark glasses and begin a sprightly jig.

"We've done it, me boy! We've done it! We've done it!"

CHAPTER TWENTY

A Word on the Subject of Risks

LATER THAT DAY—after they'd returned home and marveled at the flowers Aunt Bridget had bought; and enjoyed the extra special supper she provided, with clam chowder and four kinds of fruit to follow; and rejoiced quietly to note the new sparkle in her eyes and a fresh smoothness in her cheeks; and listened for the third or fourth time to her description of her wonderful new employer; and heard how he was "an O'Connell also, but from a very superior branch of the family and every inch of him a true gentleman"; and suffered in agonized silence the little cracks she couldn't forebear, such as, "The marvel of it is that you, James O'Connell, could never rise to such a position, coming from the same stock and all, and with something of the same looks about you, yet without the cruel handicap of the poor man's eye trouble"—after all that and when she'd gone, singing her most cheerful hymn, to take a bath, Uncle James turned to Tim and said softly, with a small grin:

"Would ya ever believe such a change could take place in a woman in so short a time?"

"She really is pleased, isn't she?" said Tim, who'd never seen her quite as happy as this before.

"Pleased? She's overjoyed, my boy! And to think we never thought of this earlier!"

"To think *I* never thought of it, you mean! It was my plan, you know."

"Yeah, but it was my execution of it that carried the day."

"Execution? That's a good word. Yeah! You nearly executed it all right. You nearly put it to death with your clowning!"

"Whisht! Whisht! She'll be hearing you above the merry bubbling of the bathwater. . . . Tell you what: It was the both of us that did it. A combined operation. Okay?"

"Go on then. . . . Okay."

"That's the smiler! Here, shake on it. Because, believe me, we have to stick together in this. United we stand, divided we fall. More than ever now."

"But you're right, Uncle. It is a pity I—er—*we* didn't think of it earlier. Instead of the sock idea, say."

"Or the millionaire," said Uncle James, his eyes lighting at the memory. "'Twas a good one though, that." Then he frowned and gently patted the table. "But as I was saying. It's gonna be trickier than ever in some ways. Like for instance how we'll always have to keep out of her way at the apartment as much as possible. You in particular."

"I know. But if we leave the key with Mr. Jenkins and her money on the piano, like you said, she need never see either of us at all."

"Well—*you* certainly, as I've just been saying. She'd better not see *you*. But me—well—suitably disguised and with the blinds down—I can't wait to be having another little discussion with her about these two slobs she says she lives with."

"Now hold it, Uncle, hold it! . . . The less you see her the less chance she'll have of recognizing you."

"Yes, well. . . . Okay, then, maybe you're right. . . . *Maybe.* . . . And of course there's our clothes—these clothes, I mean. We must always be sure to leave 'em locked up over there, out of sight, where she can't come across them by accident."

"You bet!"

"We just can't be too careful."

"No. . . . By the way . . ."

"Yes, my boy?"

"Talking about being careful, I've been meaning to ask. What did you mean by sending her across to the drapes, knowing I was right there behind them?"

Uncle James laughed softly, the chuckling noise blending perfectly with the high warbling notes of Aunt Bridget's bathtub hymn.

"Bless you, my boy, I knew it was safe! I knew there was no reason for her to be looking behind the drapes. And even if she had, your old uncle would have thought of something. Top of my form I was just then!"

"Yeah! Sure! But that's nothing to do with it. Why take unnecessary risks?"

"Risks? Risks? Necessary or unnecessary, isn't risks the spice of life, boy? Eh? Tell me that now. . . . With all this money—which was won on a risk, mark *that!*—with all this money, what is it we've done that's given you the biggest kicks?"

Tim thought for a few moments. He thought again about the sock and the "millionaire" and how *they* might have given him some pretty big kicks, if they'd succeeded. And then he thought about the traffic jam six blocks away and the storytelling episode and the superb performance given that very morning in the darkened apartment—and as he did so, his face began slowly to split open into a grin.

"Okay," he said. "You win. . . . But please, Uncle . . ." He listened and, hearing the sound of the bathwater draining away, continued rapidly in a low voice, "Please —now that we've got things set up so that Aunt Bridget can enjoy the money too—please don't let's push our luck too far, eh?"

Uncle James laughed.

"Don't you worry about that! Something tells me that with two Mr. O'Connells to handle, and your aunt dealing with them both, the risks are gonna come plenty fast enough without our seeking them!" He fumbled in one of his pockets and, causing Tim's heart to miss a beat, pulled out the false moustache. "Look, just to prove I've taken your warning to heart, my boy, I'll not be putting this on tonight, when your aunt's in the room and her back's turned, just for the fun of it, just for the thrill of living dangerously."

"I should think *not!*" gasped Tim. "You don't mean to tell me you were gonna actually put it *on?*"

"Yeah, like this. . . ."

"When she was in the room?"

"Yeah—behind her back. To give you a scare. Just for—"

"*James O'Connell! Whatever is that thing on your face?*"

Both Tim and Uncle James stood stock-still, frozen, horrified, hardly daring to look at Aunt Bridget, standing in her bathrobe and soft slippers in the doorway.

Then Uncle James came to life. He put his hand up to his mouth, touched the moustache that was held there in his puckered upper lip, kept it in place with two fingers, and said, "A bit of old black wool, my dear. I was wondering with Tim here how it would be if *I* grew a moustache like your fine new friend on Fifth Avenue. Would I be looking more like him than ever with it on?"

Aunt Bridget stared hard. She frowned. She seemed about to say something harsh. Then the new softer look returned to her face and, with a thin little smile and a sniff, she said, "Not in the least! I tell you, he's a fine distinguished-looking lawyerlike man, the kind of man as can wear a moustache without looking a fool. So take it off, James, and be content with the face God gave you."

And, with that, she went back into the bedroom, humming her hymn once more, leaving the secret winners to roll their eyes upward and wipe their foreheads and count their blessings and thank their lucky stars (not to mention their guardian angels and Nine-Day Saints) and, in general, to allow a very curious mixture of expressions —of relief, of surprise, of caution, of hope, of joy—to flit across the faces God had given them.